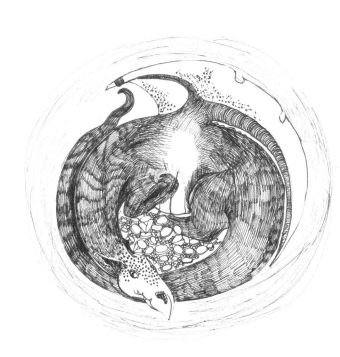

TRAVEL LIGHT

NAOMI MITCHISON

-m-
Merchiston Publishing

LIMITED EDITION

Published in 2011 by Merchiston Publishing
New Craig, Craighouse Campus, Edinburgh EH10 5LG
www.merchistonpublishing.com

Edited, designed and produced by
MSc Publishing students

ISBN: 978-0-9566136-4-6

Generously supported by the Edward Clark Trust

Printed in Scotland by Bell & Bain Ltd, Glasgow, G46 7UQ
Typeset in Bookman Old Style 11/13pt

CONTENTS

ABOUT THE AUTHOR

Lady Naomi May Margaret Mitchison was born in Edinburgh in 1897. She was a very studious child, even teaching herself Latin and Greek. She left Scotland for Oxford and went to boarding school there; the school was ominously called Dragon School. She went on to study science at Oxford University.

Mitchison volunteered as a nurse during the First World War but returned to her studies after catching scarlet fever. In 1916 she married Gilbert Richard Mitchison whilst he was on leave from Flanders, and they went on to have seven children. Sadly, their son Geoffrey died from meningitis at only nine years of age and their daughter Clemency died soon after her birth. Mitchison moved to Carradale (a 300 acre farm on the Mull of Kintyre) in 1939, where she continued to live after her husband's death in 1970, until her own in 1999.

Mitchison's first book, *The Conquered,* was written in 1923. Over the course of her career, she published more than seventy books as well as many short stories, plays and poems. These works covered several genres, from historical novels to science fiction to travel writing. She also wrote articles and reviews for *The New Statesman* and *Time and Tide,* a political and literary review magazine. In addition to writing her own works, Mitchison aided the work of others. She was a close friend of J.R.R. Tolkien (author of *The Lord of the Rings*) and played an important role in the production of this work, helping him during the proofreading process.

Mitchison had many talents and interests aside from being a writer; in 1933 she starred as a desperate housewife in the film *The Road to Hell.* She was also fiercely opposed to nuclear weapons, and campaigned against both the Nazis and Fascism. In 1952 she travelled to Moscow as part of the "Authors' World Peace Appeal". Mitchison's love of travelling also led her to Africa and Botswana, where she became a tribal advisor and tribal mother to the Bakgatla people. In addition to travel, her hobbies included botany, gardening and farming.

She cared deeply about Scotland and was involved with politics throughout her life. She first stood as a Labour candidate for the Scottish Universities in 1935. Between 1945 and 1976 she served on both the Argyll County Council and the Highlands and Islands Development Council.

Naomi Mitchison continued to write and publish into the 1990s. She died in 1999, aged 101.

*With thanks to Naomi Mitchison for
her words and to Stuart Johnston for
the right to publish them.*

PART ONE

1.

THE BEARS

t is said that when the new Queen saw the old Queen's baby daughter, she told the King that the brat must be gotten rid of at once. And the King, who by now had almost forgotten the old Queen and had scarcely looked at the baby, agreed and thought no more about it. And that would have been the end of that baby girl, but that her nurse, Matulli, came to hear of it.

Now this nurse was from Finmark, and, like many another from thereabouts, was apt to take on the shape of an animal from time to time. So she turned herself into a black bear then and there and picked up the baby in her mouth, blanket and all, and growled her way out of the Bower at the back of the King's hall. Then she padded out through the light spring snow that had melted already near the hall, and through the birch woods and the pine woods into the deep dark woods, where the rest of the bears were waking up from their winter sleep.

Now when anyone changes into a bear, it is bearish they become, and the nurse Matulli was the same. Little Halla crawled around with the bear cubs, and many a knock she got from hard claws and many a lick from rough tongues. She learnt to fight the other cubs and, having the use of her hands, she would get her own back from time to time, pulling ears and scrambling on to black backs, and sometimes she wondered when her claws would grow. She got to know the thought and language of the bears. It was a language that did what it wanted to do well enough, so that there were many ways of showing the difference between one taste and another; the taste of crunched mice, the taste of many different berries and roots and the taste of honey either on the front, back, or sides of the tongue. It did the same for smells, and the forest was always speaking in smells to the bears. It did much for hearing and something for sight, but there was no way, for instance, to think about clouds or the flying of eagles, because the bears did not look up into the sky. And if anyone had wanted to explain to the bears about Halla and her stepmother, they would just not have been able to do it at all.

There were plenty of other wild beasts in the woods; wolves and foxes and martens, reindeer and elks and roe deer and hares. But most of them kept clear of the bears. In summer, the woods were full of tangles and hollows and mosses, scented with crushed ferns, rich earth scooped for sweet shoots and young mushrooms, birds' nests full of warm eggs, and the thick friendly fur of bears. Matulli–bear looked after Halla–baby as well as any bear can be expected to look after any baby. Halla had plenty to eat, a long tongue to wash her and a warm bear to cuddle against all night. But Matulli was a fine figure of a she–bear and the he–bears all wanted her to keep house for them. It came on for winter, and behind rocks and under fallen fir trees were deep and cozy dens waiting for Matulli and her bear husband. The nights got longer and colder and every morning Matulli found it harder and harder to wake up. But Halla woke and fidgeted and pulled Matulli's whiskers and wanted her breakfast. And it came back to Matulli that one of the queer things about human beings was that they did not sensibly sleep all winter, but instead went to a great deal of trouble to cut fuel and shear sheep and weave blankets and thick cloaks and make themselves hot soup. And Halla, in spite of her excellent upbringing, was going to take after the rest of them. What was a poor bear to do?

And then a very fortunate thing happened. Matulli and her bear husband were walking through the woods, looking for the last of the wild bees' honey or a late fledgling from a nest, and Matulli's husband was grumbling away to himself because he could feel that the snow was not far off and it was time to go home to the den and sleep and sleep. But Halla was running around like a crazy butterfly and clearly had no intention of sleeping. Sometimes the he–bear thought it would be both nice and sensible to eat Halla, but he did not dare because of Matulli.

And suddenly a deer came galloping past them, looking back over its shoulder in a terrible fright. And after that a badger, which was in a hurry too. But the badger had time to tell the two bears that there was a dragon coming along and they had better get out of the way. The he–bear turned round at once and went galumphing back; never had his den seemed so desirable. But Matulli sat back among the cranberry bushes in the wet moss and pulled Halla down beside her. Sure enough, in a little while the dragon came along, puffing and creaking and rattling. Matulli in the bushes coughed and said, "my Lord". For she knew in her mind that dragons appreciated politeness from the rest of the world.

This dragon was somewhat startled and blew out a flame which singed the tops of the cranberry bushes and the tips of the fur all along Matulli's back. But he had meant no harm, and he stopped and listened very graciously to Matulli's story about Halla Bearsbairn. Matulli was speaking in the language of humans, since the thing could not be explained in bears' language. But dragons are, within their limits, very intelligent; most of them understand not only the language of several kinds of animals (including the birds who have beautiful feelings but few facts), but also the languages of trolls, dwarves, giants and human beings.

Now, if there is one kind of human being which dragons dislike more than another, it is the kind commonly called kings or heroes. The reason is that they are almost always against dragons. So when the dragon, whose name was Uggi, heard that the poor little pink human had been so badly treated by a king and a queen, he did not hesitate, but said at once that he would adopt Halla Bearsbairn and see that she grew up in all the right principles of dragonhood. "And you will see that she gets regular meals, my Lord?" said Matulli.

"Have you ever heard of dragons going hungry?" said Uggi.

"And you will see that she doesn't fall into the fire, my Lord?"

"I will fire–proof her myself," the dragon said.

"And you will comb her hair every night, my Lord?"

"I will comb it with my own claws," said the dragon, "for I see that the child has hair the colour of gold, which is the only right colour for hair."

"And you will dry her eyes when she cries, my Lord?"

"I will dry her eyes with the silken scarf of the Princess of the Spice Lands who was so thoughtfully offered to my cousin, the Dragon of the Great Waste. For I see that the child has eyes the colour of sapphires, which is the only right colour for eyes."

"What happened to the Princess of the Spice Lands, my Lord?" asked Matulli, for she thought that this princess might be a nice playmate for her Halla.

The dragon coughed behind his claw. "The Princess of the Spice Lands was offered to my cousin by the populace. It was a very suitable and acceptable idea on their part. Unfortunately there was a hero sent to interfere with everybody's best interests. In the result the princess — *and* the hero — perished. My poor cousin had a nasty jag over one eye. He gave me the scarf in exchange for a duplicate bracelet that I had acquired. Yes, yes." And Uggi the dragon held out a glittering claw to Halla who caught hold and swung.

"And you'll see she's warm at night, my Lord?" said Matulli, anxious to do her duty but thinking more and more pleasantly of the comfortable den and the uninterrupted sleep that waited for her.

"She will be quite warm, and what is more," said the dragon, "she will always have a night–light, because I am proud to say that we dragons always breathe out of our noses while we are asleep." He then put Halla up on to his back, where she held on by the spikes and shouted with pleasure because now she could see right up into the trees.

Suddenly, the thought of her den and her husband and her long sleep was too much for Matulli–bear and she tried to curtsey to the dragon, but that is too difficult for bears. So she just turned her large black back and went crashing back through the cranberry bushes and into the forest. Uggi the dragon raised his eyebrows and looked over his shoulder at Halla and winked slowly from the side of his eye across, in the same way that a crocodile winks, and then quickly up and down, the same way as an eagle, for he had something of the nature of both.

But Halla was delighted with it all and dug her bare heels into the scaly sides of the dragon, who went slithering and crackling off through the forest, every now and then accidentally setting fire to a bush or a drift of dry birch or oak leaves, or singeing the fur of one of the animals which was too proud or too stupid to get out of the way.

2.

THE DRAGONS

 n his way home that evening, Uggi took a short flight to the top of Signal Hill, whose summit was all scorched and scarred so that not even the stillest stones grew moss on them. Here he gave a great blast and flames like enormous golden lilies shot out of his nostrils and vanished into sudden dusk. His cousins — Bauk, Gork, Hafr and Hroar — came flying over, creaking with their wings like a thousand flights of geese. They were told the whole story, while Halla Bearsbairn drummed her bare feet on her own dragon's back. Very sensibly, they decided to fire–proof her at once, before anything awkward could happen.

The ceremony of fire–proofing is a very old and beautiful one, which can only be performed by the Goddess Demeter or by not less than three members of the Ancient Order of Dragons, of whom at least one must be a Master Dragon. Halla, who was used to being licked by bears' tongues, thought nothing of being licked by the forked–flame tongues of dragons. For a short while afterwards everything that she looked at appeared to have a fine fringe of flame; indeed this would come back to her afterwards, when she was much older, if ever she got angry.

All that evening and far into the night and long after Halla was asleep, the dragons moved and danced round her in an earnest excitement, spiring up from Signal Hill towards the stars, shooting out bursts of flame which reflected from polished scales and claws and multiplied themselves into hundreds of flashes and twinkles. Sometimes they would spring into the air, clapping their wings together and undulating downwards. Sometimes they would shoot away till they were as tiny as rockets and then come thundering back. And they determined that they would bring up the maiden Halla to do credit to every kind of dragonhood and to be a bane to kings and heroes and all such enemies of true dragons. And carefully, before morning greyed the night sky, or dimmed the frosty stars, Uggi the Master Dragon carried back the sleeping child in his great claws, and her pale gold hair swished and feathered in the flame of his breathing, but was never singed.

And so Halla was brought up by the dragons, and year after year she learnt to think of things in the dragonish way. She had long lessons, specialising in geology, arithmetic and especially multiplication, which led in turn to economics, always an important part of dragon history, and also of course in such elements of magic as were thought suitable for her. When lessons were over she was allowed to play with Uggi's treasure, go sliding down heaps of pearls and build towers of gold and ivory boxes. She could dress herself up in ropes of jewels and look at herself for as long as she liked in polished silver mirrors; these were held up for her by an admiring young dragon with a fiery smile but only recently hatched and still soft–scaled. She wore cloth of gold, or cloth of silver when she went blackberrying. For, try as the dragons would to get rid of such tastes, she was bearish about berries and honey. Still, she learnt to enjoy dinner parties of over–roasted joints, chops grilled hard, blazing plum puddings and ginger snaps. And of course she had as much snapdragon as she liked.[1]

Dragons like to live on blasted heaths and desolate, snow–capped, igneous mountains, but Bork or Hafr, who were young dragons, not many centuries old, would often take her for rides down to the deep woods or the rivers and, from a distance, they would point out to her the dwellings of men, the halls with the fields and barns and stockades round them at the head of the fjords, and the boats moored at the jetties or drawn up on land in times of storm. The

---

1. In case you have never eaten snapdragon this is how it is made. You get a shallow metal tray (real dragons always have gold) and you scatter blanched almonds and raisin clusters on it, then you pour brandy all over and set it alight. Then you pull out and eat as many almonds and raisins as you can. As I remember it, there used to be a lot of nasty juice left at the end, but it is more than forty years since I ate it last, for people have forgotten to honour the dragons.

biggest of these were called dragon ships, but the dragons themselves were never certain how to take this. It might, of course, and properly should be, a form of worship, but with the race of men one never knew.

In summer, Dragon Mountain was hot and stuffy and the Desolate Heath made prickly walking. But in winter, all was snow–covered and the enormous northern lights drew curtains of shimmer between earth and upper air or stilt–danced round the Pole Star. The dragons rushed through them, crackling with static. In winter, too, they heard the Fenris Wolf howling, far, far away, yet too near for comfort. But Halla knew that nothing could hurt her so long as she was with the rest of the dragons and diligently guarding a treasure.

In her history lessons she learnt, first, about the beginnings of things, the tree Yggdrasil growing above the first dragon's nest, before the first dragons had chipped their milky eggs, about the weaving of the Norns and the peculiar habits and preferences of All–Father, who had made men in order to amuse himself. And then she learnt about the rebellion of men against dragons; how men had been taught by the Great Dragon to keep sheep and cows for dragon dinners and not to complain if an occasional shepherd was eaten with his flocks, since that was all to the good when looked at the right way. When flocks and herds increased and over–production was threatened, dragons stepped (or more usually flew) into the breach and disposed of the surplus with no trouble at all. Occasionally, and for everyone's good, mankind were instructed to offer a fresh and juicy princess to their own particular dragon. It was said that the princesses enjoyed the experience. Certainly the dragons did.

But mankind became rebellious. Kings and champions and heroes, unfairly armed with flame–resisting armour and unpleasant lances, were encouraged by certain underground elements and against the wishes and interests of the bulk of the population, to interfere between princess and dragon. Occasionally this resulted in tragedies, as in the case of the good dragon who was killed by the man George, or of the dragon so cruelly done to death by Perseus when about to make the acquaintance of Andromeda. It could be verified that no princess was ever asked whether she wanted to be rescued and carried off by a dragon–slayer to a fate (no doubt) worse than death. Sometimes, too, a dragon was murdered in cold blood, as happened quite recently to the dragon Fafnir, an uncle of Gauk's and a Master Dragon, who was rudely awakened and brutally stabbed by a young man called Siegfried, who, however, came to no good end himself.

But more often in the stories, the dragon made good and all ended for the best. Sometimes Halla played at Princesses and Dragons, pretending to be tied to a tree and then waiting for one of the young dragons to rush at her with his mouth open, drenching her in delightful, tickly flames. And there would be no horrible hero to interfere. Sometimes Halla found herself wishing she was a real princess, so that it could all genuinely happen.

But the economics were more serious. Briefly, they came to this. The dragons gathered gold. The kings and heroes squandered it. Among kings, the shocking name of praise was bracelet–giver. And from where did the golden bracelets come? Why, from the treasure that some dragon had painstakingly amassed, with what care and thought and industry! Then, in some low way, a dragon would be attacked and murdered and the gold dispersed into the hands of those who had done nothing to earn it. Heroes prided themselves on a thing called generosity. And what was generosity? It was the giving away of something to those that had not earned it, and it was usually done *by* those that had not earned it.

What sentiment or practice could be more revolting to dragons of right feeling? It would then be necessary for the robbed dragon to go over the whole process of collecting, storing away and cataloguing and finally guarding — even with his life, remember! — a new treasure. Every dragon had his cave and, in the order of nature, every cave had its treasure; for was not the sparkle of treasure implicit in the velvet darkness of a cave? This was part of the order and pattern of life, as laid down since the beginning of time.

"Where does the gold come from *first*?" asked Halla, frowning over it, sitting there on a rock with her hands round her knees and her golden, dragon–combed hair pouring down over her cloth of gold school frock with the great rubies round the neck and weighting the hem.

"It is melted out of the rocks by the dwarves," said Uggi, "and in the old days it was only the dwarves who could work it. But now unfortunately they have taught the art to men. Yet it was always the men who won it from the dwarves by force and trickery, which is the kind of thing mankind is clever at. And it is always through men that it comes to its home and safe–keeping in some dragon's cave."

"Why don't the dragons get it straight from the dwarves?" asked Halla, "then there needn't be men."

"Because," said Uggi patiently, "dwarves live in cracks and holes into which dragons, being of a proper size, cannot get. But men, being halfway to dwarves, wriggle in after them."

Halla stretched her arms and the bracelets clinked and the rings flashed in the sunshine. "I'm glad I'm a dragon," she said.

"Never forget, child," said old Uggi, "not only to think dragon thoughts, but also that you are part of a dragon's treasure. My treasure. And remember, if a man were to see you, he would immediately try to steal everything you are wearing and carry it away and probably murder you as well."

"I'd breathe fire on him." said Halla. "When will you teach me to breathe fire? I'm tired of history."

"It is very sad," said Uggi, "but I cannot teach you to breathe fire."

"Why not?" asked Halla. "Is it because I was a bear once? If only you would show me how to breathe fire, I would try to stop eating berries and getting my paws full of earth!" For the dragons were always speaking to her about these habits.

Uggi sighed, a hot, hot sigh that burnt a small patch of lichen that had survived so far on the side of the rock. He felt that, in spite of the way he had brought Halla up as a dragon, the moment was come when she must learn the facts of life, hard though it would be for him to tell them to her. He went on, "it is time, my child, that I told you something. Have you noticed, when you look at yourself in the shining mirror, that you are not like me nor indeed like any of the dragons?"

"Not *very* like," said Halla, admiring her long toes, which were decorated with gold and emerald toe–rings, but which were not quite long enough, nor nearly sharp enough for claws. "Perhaps I shall be more like you when I am older. I think I can feel my wings growing," she added, looking backwards over her shoulder and scratching her back.

Uggi the dragon wept a sizzling tear. "My child, I am afraid you will never grow to look like a dragon, for the truth is, you are not a dragon."

"But—" said Halla, and her lip trembled, "I feel like a dragon. You always tell me I'm a dragon. Oh, I know I'm a dragon!"

"Alas!" said Uggi. "That is not enough. Though it is something. I am afraid that what I have to say will upset you very much, my dear. You must be brave, brave as a good dragon. The truth is that you are a child of man and only by adoption one of us. But never mind," he said eagerly, "you are quite safe. You shall never go back to them. Unless, that is, you want to do so."

Halla burst into tears and threw her arms round Uggi's neck. "I could never possibly want to go back, never!" she said. "Why did you have to tell me? Why can't you turn me into a dragon?"

"Even the Norns, or All–Father himself, could not do that," said Uggi gravely.

"But why not?" asked Halla. "You taught me magic. I can make magic frogs out of stones, after all! Can't I?" It was one of her best–learned lessons in magic.

"But think," said Uggi. "Those frogs only do what you want. Unless you say the Word to them, they cannot jump. If I were to turn you into a dragon — and I very much doubt if I could — you would only be able to fly or breathe fire or gather treasure or do any other dragonish thing if I said the Word to you. You would not be a dragon in your own mind and heart — in the way, my dear, that I believe you are now!" And he planted a fiery kiss on her forehead, and then bethought himself of an ancient carved emerald at the very back of his treasure cave, which Halla had never seen. They would go and find it together. So she cheered up, for she was dragon–minded enough to find the thought of treasure above all elevating.

3.

VISITORS ON DRAGON MOUNTAIN

s she grew older, the fact of being a human weighed on her less. Often she forgot it for days at a time. Once, they were visited by the Grendel family — curious–shaped and rather watery folk who looked askance at Halla because she reminded them of the awful fate that had befallen their grandmother and their elder uncle, at the hands of the man Beowolf, who had actually followed the poor old lady right into her house at the bottom of the Terrible Mere and cut off her arm. And all because they had punctually taken their tribute — and no more — from the hall of the King of Denmark. It made you wonder what the world was coming to. It made you suspect anyone of humanity. But soon they realised that Halla was not that kind of human, and when they said goodbye, leaving wet marks on the stones of Dragon Mountain, where they had been sitting, they had been so delighted with Halla's sympathy and anger that they suggested she should be called Halla Heroesbane. They were sure that she would be

the means of avenging dragons and Grendels and such on the race of heroes, and a proud girl was Halla that night, curling up to sleep in her nest of moss and pearls, half–bearish and half–dragonish. Bearsbairn had been a good name to start with, since it distinguished her from all other humans, but Heroesbane was better.

News would come to Dragon Mountain of events in the significant world, which was not of course the world of men, nor yet of Gods. Dragon events took place on various levels. There was, for instance, the lighting of the centennial pyre which the phoenix constructed for herself; a young, untreasured dragon would be chosen to perform the ceremony with a single, well–directed puff. This always meant a gathering of noble and ancient dragons in the Arabian waste. Uggi had been there once in his early days. But now he was apt to think of such things as superfluities; his heart was where his treasure was. But Halla enjoyed hearing about these things and would have liked to take part in the rejoicings; she pictured herself sometimes as the superb, white–hot phoenix, but more often as the modest young dragon whose one deed had been perfectly done, presage of a solid and splendid future.

From time to time Uggi would go off on business. He would see that his claws were sharp and his wing–joints supple, and Halla would look over his scales to make sure that none of them were cracked or in need of repair. If they were, she would take out her file and polish and her little box of practical magic and soon set everything to rights. It was a great help to Uggi. But she always worried about the soft patch behind his foreleg, and once she tried to get him to wear a neat little piece of chain armour there. She had found it among the treasure and thought it was just the thing. Uggi, however, condemned it out of hand as undragonish and told her firmly that there was no danger. And indeed, sooner or later, back he would come with an addition to the family plate. Delightedly Halla would date and catalogue it, and between them they would find just the right niche in the rocks of the treasure cave, in which it would rest.

While Uggi was away, Halla would do her homework, and the younger dragons would look in for tea, which, of course, they took as nearly as possible on the boil, with red–pepper sandwiches. Sometimes other creatures from the country beyond the deep forest would come, including various unicorns which would keep on following Halla about and soppily laying their heads down in her lap whenever she sat down, and eyeing her with their great golden eyes. As their heads were very heavy, this was a nuisance, especially when two of them did it together. Nor were they anything like so much fun to ride as the dragons.

Sometimes the spongy–nosed trolls came, but instead of talking properly they made hollow noises like caves, and they dropped bones about. Then there were the giants, many of whom had peculiarities, such as a third eye, of which they were so proud that they could never stop talking about them, while others bragged about seven–league boots and cloaks of invisibility, which always looked very ordinary. There was the great Boygg who carried a pine tree for an umbrella and with one motion of his thumb opened it out into an oak if it looked like rain. But he always talked in riddles, which made Halla feel very shy. And none of them took a really serious sensible view about treasure; in fact, the trolls often made stupid jokes about it, in the worst taste.

Once Bork took her to visit the old sea serpent who wore a crown on each head and talked slobberingly with all of them at once so that Halla became quite confused. She met some attractive young mermaids that day though, and found that several of them had already achieved her ambition and put down one or two heroes. But when she asked them how it had been done there was very nearly a nasty accident — they said they would show her, and before she knew where she was they had pulled her into the bottom of a pool and were holding her under, laughing streams of bubbles. Indeed, they only let her go when Bork, who suddenly realised what was happening, began to bite their tails. Perhaps the mermaids had not meant any harm, but Halla was quite upset and refused to go near the sea again.

It was during one of these business absences of Uggi's, when Halla was by herself on Dragon Mountain polishing the jewels, that a thunderstorm burst almost overhead, and right out of the centre of the blackest cloud bounced a winged horse who came down with all four hoofs together almost on Uggi's doorstep and struck fire out of the rock. He was a strong, hairy–hocked, broad–backed, thick–necked, hog–maned horse with coarse wing feathers, and he had need to be strong because the young woman on his back was the kind that could have pushed over a haystack with one hand. And indeed she needed to be, for she was a Valkyrie and often she had to pick up a young hero with a spear through him at full gallop, and throw him over her crupper, or carry him under one arm up to Valhalla, and that at a time when he could do nothing to help himself. The young woman dismounted, took her helmet off so that the red hair rolled out from under it in two great plaits, scratched herself through her chain mail and asked, "Have you such a thing as a needle and thread, child? My petticoat's gone again."

Halla, who suspected from her manner that she was one of the All–Father's wish children, hurried to bring her what she needed. While the Valkyrie, whose name was Steinvor, mended her gathers, taking big stitches and occasionally pricking her finger and swearing, they chatted. Halla apologised for having nothing to give the horse; Steinvor herself had taken a cup of mead. "We can't grow anything up here," she said, "not so much as a crowberry. Everything gets singed sooner or later."

"So I should suppose," said Steinvor. "And you wouldn't catch me waiting here a week. Steady, boy, steady; whoa there!" she called to her horse, which was fidgeting. "He can't stand the smell of dragons," she explained.

"Dragons have no smell!" said Halla indignantly.

"That's what you think, my dear," said Steinvor, wrinkling her nose, "but I can tell you, it's rank. Look, why don't you walk out? Oh, I don't mean going back to mankind, it's easy to see that's not your line. But there's my game. Why not join the girls? I'll speak to All–Father myself. And it's a great life."

"Thank you very much," said Halla politely, "but I don't think I'd like it. You're always choosing heroes, aren't you — touching them? And I hate them!"

"They don't always appreciate being chosen!" said Steinvor, and laughed a short loud laugh, like a horse. "We pick them off before they've had time to do all they'd like. But All–Father's going to need every one of them when it comes to the Last Battle, and meanwhile they can think they're leading the life they're accustomed to. Anyhow, who cares about them? The game is, picking them out. It beats pig–sticking every time."

"You bring them in to help All–Father in the fight against the Midgard Serpent?" said Halla doubtfully. "Of course, I haven't actually met the Midgard Serpent—"

"Ahha!" said Steinvor. "And you don't know which side you're on, you and your dragons! I see, I see!" And she jabbed Halla in the ribs with the butt–end of her dagger — she was cleaning her nails with the point of it.

"The dragons always speak most respectfully of All–Father," said Halla, anxious not to say the wrong thing.

"So they might, so they might," said Steinvor. "I'm not at all certain, all the same, whether or not they're on All–Father's side. They're probably related to the Midgard Serpent. And you don't want to be caught on the wrong foot, do you? Come along with me, child; the horse is used to carrying two. I'll speak to All–Father, it'll be quite all right—" And she seized Halla by the arm and began hauling her over to the horse like a land girl with a calf.

"No!" screamed Halla. "No, I don't want to — I'm a dragon—"

"Nonsense," said Steinvor, and almost got Halla on to the horse when she gave a twist, bit like a dragon, clawed like a bear and attacked Steinvor's petticoat gathers, which, as she knew, were the vulnerable part. Steinvor, unused to being attacked by those she carried off, who were still usually so surprised at having been killed that they never moved a finger, let Halla go.

"I'm ashamed of you, child," she said, "wanting to live with smelly dragons when you might be in Valhalla. I don't know what the Norns will think, I'm sure, but I shall certainly tell them." And she kicked her heels into her horse's side and bounced back into her stormcloud with a great clap of thunder that echoed through all the mountains.

Poor Halla sat down and cried. If the Valkyrie meant it and the Norns were to alter her fate! And which side were the dragons on? And did they smell? Hroar, who was a reddish–green dragon with snaggly front teeth, came sailing up. She asked him, cautiously, whether he knew which side the dragons would be on at the last battle. "We shall be on the winning side, of course," said Hroar.

"But will that be All–Father's side?"

"Don't bother your head about all that," said Hroar, coiling himself affectionately round her rock. "All–Father goes back to the beginning. So do the dragons. What comes from the beginning will be there at the end. Have some of these Gods been worrying you? Was it that Loki?"

"No — no — "

"I saw a nasty little rainbow at the far side of Blasted Heath — did one of them come running down? You'd know All–Father, wouldn't you?" he whispered smokily. "Walks around in disguise with his hat over one eye, pretending to be a Wanderer, but there's always something about him. And he goes around with two ravens — can't trust them. It's said they're on the side of men — reminding him of what's best forgotten — and the same with Baldur and Thor. But we mustn't think too much about it: we must be brave and stick to what we know, to being dragons. You're not crying, are you?"

"No," said Halla, gulping. "I know what's right."

4.

THE HERO

o things went on, and Halla ceased worrying about what the Norns might or might not have been told. They did not appear to be doing anything different to the web of her destiny. Perhaps, after all, Steinvor had no access to the Norns, no knowledge of the tree Yggdrasil, nor indeed of much else which might go on under All–Father's hat. And slowly Uggi's treasure grew and the treasure cave was further hollowed out, Uggi working with claws, Halla with paws. Sometimes they would visit other dragons and inspect their treasures, and Uggi would advise the young dragons to be careful and systematic in their taking of tribute and, even though there appeared to be a superabundance in the fields of mankind, to make use, not only of flocks and herds, but also of reindeer and elk and such. But, in case it might hurt Halla's feelings, none of them mentioned the edibility of bears by dragons.

But if dragons have a fault — and they will laughingly admit that this is so — it is a certain graspingness, an inability to compromise. And it was probably this tendency in Ljot, one of the young dragons, which led to the rebellion when, first, he was refused his tribute, and then, when the people of the Dales, his particular subjects, had been successful in this, the anti–dragon movement spread to others. This began when, instead of driving one or two choice oxen up to the rocky edge of the pastures and then hurriedly retreating, the men began to drive their herds back into caves with bars across their mouths or even stone–built byres. When Ljot, not a very large or experienced dragon, and indeed less than two hundred years old, attempted to take his tribute, a number of men with spears ran at him, shouting very rudely, and he had barely time to take off.

One of the difficulties of mankind is that they have the vice of inventiveness. It would be an easier world for dragons if this were not so, or if it could be kept within bounds, used for the better working of gold, setting of jewels, or such trading activities as bringing treasure from far countries within reach of dragons. Instead, mankind develops against all dragon interests. Instead of wattle and wooden palisades, which are bad enough, they build in stone. Their swords become sharper, their armour more effective. When Uggi was a young dragon, as he had often told Halla, there was poking of sharpened stakes which, all the same, might hurt cruelly. Shields were of hide. Swords were of bronze, but unless by some unusual accident, it was seldom necessary to come into close contact with them. Arrows were seldom effective, although they were bronze–pointed; whereas in Uggi's grandfather's time there had been nothing but flint and bone points.

But now swords were of iron and much sharper and stronger. Spears had bronze or iron blades, were much longer and more unpleasant. Bows and arrows were heavier and could do serious injury. Armour was disconcertingly flame–resistant. In fact, dragons were practically defenceless in a cruel world.

Still, one must persevere. The other dragons advised Ljot to start ravening; if necessary, to fly in the early morning and pick up a child or two who might have run out of the house before the men were about. Or a woman going out to milk. This should be effective in recalling his subjects to their duty. If the King of the Dales happened to have a daughter of suitable age and edibility, it could be suggested that she would be an acceptable offering. Ljot would then be able to take it easy again and all would be well.

Ljot, however, must have blundered, or underestimated the barbarity and ingenuity of his subjects. Instead of a plump daughter, the King of the Dales had a scraggy and muscular son. There was coming and going, a trap laid — a fat bullock, a hook. It was all very distressing. Ljot should have been more careful. When it was over, the other dragons divided up Ljot's treasure according to the old rules, and held a council. Although he kept it from Halla, Uggi was uneasy, more uneasy than he had been in all his long life.

The Council of Dragons met for a full night on Signal Hill. From far to the north and east dragons glided and undulated in, long glitters and streaks wavering past the still stars and thin half hoop of moon. The further dragons were strangely bewhiskered and tentacled; some wore nightcaps or shawls of mist. The oldest spoke only in proverbs of admitted wisdom but not applicable to the present situation. The various Master Dragons gave their opinions, backed by examples out of history. A necessarily successful policy was bound to follow from the correct working out of well–known economic rules. The only difficulty was that mankind was not conforming to them. There were arguments on the tightening or loosening of custom and quoting of precedents. Should there, for instance, be a mass attack by dragons on the people of the Dales? If so, it might be a salutary and much–needed lesson to mankind, but it was only too probable that valuable dragon power might be sacrificed. Certainly there would be great unpleasantness. Again, if dragons from the further parts were to be called upon, it would certainly be necessary to provide feasts: not merely venison and such, but the best of everything, including the stores of ginger, pepper, hot spices and potent distillations acquired with such industry and often at the cost of long and wing–exhausting flights far from the comforts of home. It might even be necessary to divide up certain treasures. This was only hinted at, but it caused contractions of heart to those nearer dragons, whose laboriously earned savings of centuries might be required of them. Uggi thought painfully of a certain golden cup, incised with runes and the shape of ships, which had been much admired and would certainly be demanded as his contribution. He thought of the necklace of flat–cut rubies, which he had acquired from the King of Laxwater, who must in turn have got it in distant trading. He thought of several great lumps of polished amber, two of them set in gold. It would break his heart if these had to be given up. Surely it would be better to allow the men of Dales to triumph for a while, to grow careless as they most certainly would do, and then for Ljot's successor — and there were some promising young dragons at the Council — to assert himself.

At dawn the Council broke up, after a feast which sadly depleted the stores of the home dragons. A second night produced no better results. The eastern dragons began to complain of the cold, the northern dragons of the heat. After a flight of investigation, Hafr reported that the unfortunate Ljot had been ignominiously skinned and stuffed. When Uggi came home, tired and dispirited, Halla asked anxiously how things had gone and when Uggi explained, her bearish nature arose and she demanded to be allowed to go and revenge Ljot herself. She had hunted through the treasure and found herself a magnificent gold inlaid helmet and shield, and a golden–collared mail shirt of great lightness.

The pommel of her sword was encrusted with splendid jewels, and her dirk the same. She was big enough now to find the sword pleasant and easy to her hand and arm. "If you have named me Halla Heroesbane, then let me be bane to heroes, and let me begin now!" she said.

But Uggi was shocked and told her that lady dragons (who are in any case rare) stay at home and guard the treasure. Now this is an ancient dragon fallacy, since in fact the lady dragons are very much fiercer than any other, especially when they have a nest full of eggs. And (although this is always denied) lady dragons have been known to kill and eat other dragons and, what is worse, to take their treasures. Perhaps Uggi was most upset at the idea that Halla should risk some of his treasure in an adventure which might turn out badly. He refused to carry her on his back, as she begged him to do, to the Dales, and he forbade Hafr or Gauk or any of them from doing so, however much she might ask them.

He told her, however, of one thing which had been discussed at the Council of Dragons. It was said by some that at Micklegard on the Middle Sea was the greatest treasure in the world, constantly added to by ships and armies, and this must of necessity and according to all the rules of history and economics, be the possession of some great and noble dragon. Nobody knew what or who dwelt in the jasper and porphyry chambers and behind the gold and peacock curtains of Micklegard. "Some day," said Uggi, "I will take you, my child, to visit the Great Dragon of Micklegard, for I am certain that such a being must live there."

Again the night streamed with dragons streaking homeward. Nothing had been decided upon. Perhaps it would not happen again. None of the others mentioned Ljot and soon even Halla forgot him. And sooner or later, of course, everything turned out as the Master Dragons had foretold in their wisdom. The men of the Dales grew proud and careless, decided that there had never been more than one dragon and they had killed him, and so began to send their growing flocks and herds further afield into the woods and clearings towards the deep forest and the mountains. In fact, it now became apparent that they would soon reach a state of over–production, and it was time that some dragon stepped in. Neither Gauk nor Hroar, who were the nearest dragons, were very anxious to be the first. It was true that the son of the King of the Dales had decorated himself and his friends with golden bracelets which would be useful and appropriate additions to any treasure; but they also prided themselves as casters of spears, and bowmen, and, if they could catch a running deer in the heart, or a wild boar, or a wolf, how much more dangerous for the large target area of a dragon, especially for that defenceless and ticklish part behind the foreleg!

There was now a war between the men of the Dales and the men of Axewater, in the course of which, (so the dragons were informed by a troll who had taken his family down to the battle ground in order to picnic on the remains), considerable booty had passed, including an ivory drinking horn set with gold (which in turn had been captured in a ship raid to the south by the Axewater men) and a king's high seat of carved wood inlaid with various kinds of precious metal and enamel. It seemed to Uggi that his collection had long lacked an ivory drinking horn, which might easily be lost or broken during the careless and drunken feastings of men. True, there was a certain risk in obtaining it, but what worthy enterprise is without risk?

Uggi began to prepare himself. Halla begged him to take her with him; she had practiced all kinds of sword and spear work. He refused. At last she said crossly that it was time she started having a treasure of her own. And that excellent sentiment certainly made Uggi think. But he became increasingly certain that this time he must go alone. If his nestling Halla were to start a treasure (and perhaps it was only right that she should do so, although few actual dragons did so before the end of their first century) then it must not start with the gold and ivory drinking horn from the Great Hall of the Dales. That was to be his own.

So away flew Uggi with all the wisdom of his many years of dragonhood and the wind creaking in his wings. And back he trailed the next day — one wing dragging, blood drops trailing after him, and the haft of a spear broken in the soft part of his side behind the foreleg. Halla did what she could, but her little box of magic was no use here, nor her tears. Poor Uggi lay limp and chilly, his vital fire half quenched, his throat choked with cinders. And the day after they saw below them, at the foot of Dragon Mountain, a brutal gang of plunderers, led by the son of the King of the Dales, who was now openly being called hero and dragon–slayer by his companions. It was a terrible sight, and as they climbed relentlessly over the rocks, following the blood trail, Halla helped Uggi deep into the cave, and herself, set and furious, put on her armour and took up her sword. Uggi groaned and bled. She put her arms round his neck, but now he scarcely noticed; now with so little time left to him he concentrated on essentials; what truly mattered was his treasure. He signalled to her feebly to spread his wings over it, to arrange his head so that he could at least scorch his first assailant with whatever flame was left in him.

Weeping, Halla did what he wanted and then rushed bear–like down the slope at the oncoming assailants. In her anger everything appeared flame–fringed. She wounded one before she was herself disarmed, knocked down, her gold–collared mail shirt stripped off her by practiced hands, and her hands tied. They left her on the ground, growling with fury and frustration. She did not see the death of Uggi, only the blast and dimming whistle of the last flame frothing out of him and then the murderers coming staggering from the cave, their arms full of treasure.

Then she was dragged along to the fire they had lit and on which they were cooking a meal. The son of the King of the Dales had now, although somewhat scorched and grimed, decked himself out with gold — the bracelets and collars she knew and loved so well! — and was giving it away to his followers just as she had always been told was the way of men. He looked at her, grinning, and asked her what she was called; she named herself Halla Bearsbairn, since she could not, for shame, speak her other name now. "It is clear you know the way of bears," said the King's son, "and after supper I shall teach you the way of women." So he drove his spear into the rock and Halla was tied to it by her long, gold-coloured hair. During supper they threw bones at her while she wept for Uggi and herself. Here she was, tied like the princesses in the stories, but alas, for no dragon. As dusk fell, one of the unicorns came softly up behind and sadly laid its velvet muzzle in the palm of her bound hand as though saying goodbye. A troll family crept on their knobbled knees into the cave and she knew they were going to gorge themselves on fresh dragon meat. And now the wine that the robbers had brought with them was going down their throats in great gulps. And now the son of the King of the Dales stood up, while the rest shouted and sang such words as are used on these occasions toward heroes, and he came towards Halla like a hungry bear towards a broken-legged fawn.

But, as Halla screamed in expectation of his touch, there came a roaring in the sky, oh nearing, circling, making pause to all below it, a thunder of wings, a lambent, a searing of flame, a forked tail sweeping the hero off his unsteady feet, a snap of jaws through ashen spear shaft, a clutch of claws, and Halla at the last moment, rescued by a dragon!

5.

TREASURE

 t was Gauk, faithful to his old friend and cousin, who had rescued Halla. He carried her, fainting, in his strong claws, to Withered Wood, where among scorched and lifeless tree–boles and ashes of leaf and turf, he had his cave and his treasure (though it was not so great a treasure as Uggi's). Dutifully, Halla admired it, but with a dry and shaken heart. Her own treasure of sword, helmet, dagger and mail shirt, had been taken from her; her fingers and wrists were still sore where the heroes had stripped her of rings and bracelets. They had not seen a fine gold chain round her neck, dangling a carved jewel, but she thought it best to give this to Gauk.

A little later, when the men were safely away, they ventured back. There was a little left in the darker cracks of the cave; a few pearls, a ruby ring, some thin gold coins half–grown over with moss, a broken bracelet and a walrus–ivory box wrenched open and thrown aside. Such as it was, this treasure was divided between the cousins

49

of Uggi. Halla would have liked something, but it was not offered. Half in, half out of the cave were the remains of Uggi himself. But what the trolls had left the wolves had taken. There was little left but rags of skin, the toothed skull, the claws. Halla took up one of the claws and hid it in the fold of her torn cloth of gold dress. And she thought to herself that now she should be Halla Dragonweeper. And all of a sudden she remembered the Great Dragon of Micklegard and it came into her mind that sooner or later she must go to Micklegard herself.

After a while she spoke of it to Gauk, but he knew no more than the rest. Only he warned her that it would be necessary to go through the lands of men and it might be that she could not avoid meeting a hero or such. She began to ask herself what she should do, for her life appeared to have been cracked across and in some way she did not feel so dragon–minded as she had done in Uggi's time. It was as though the murderers who had killed the old dragon had also killed a dragonishness in herself and she hated them all the more for it. Or could it be that the Norns, having been informed, had taken to a different spinning of her fate? She practised such small pieces of magic as had been taught to her, but they were all childish and useless. Few of the dragons knew the great magic.

For a while she had a mind to go back to the bears, and looked for them in the forest, but, although she could join with them comfortably in hunting for bees' nests or mushroom glades, there was not much else they could do together. They did not even sing to the moon as the wolves did. Was Matulli, her nurse, still among them? If so, Matulli had grown so bear–minded that she had forgotten her nurseling, and Halla could not now remember the smell of Matulli–bear that had once meant so much to her.

For another while she wandered in the forest; living on eggs and mice, berries and nuts and roots, bears' food. She talked to all the birds and beasts whose language she knew; but their lives lacked seriousness, and above all memory, and she was used to the centuries of the dragons in which each year might be memorable for something gained and in which there were long–laid plans for the furthering of the right order of things between dragons and mankind. Birds did not have memories; although memory had them, forcing them blindly and willingly into strange actions, sending them on journeys of many thousand miles and through every kind of danger, or fixing air routes to and from their nests so that, if the nests were moved only a short way, memory would relentlessly keep them from even so much change as would save their chilling eggs and nestlings. That was no world for Halla, even though it might be full of immediate bodily emotions which memory translated into delightful action and enchanting song. The dragons did not sing and Halla had never sung. But now she would mimic the birds, trying to repeat and answer their memory songs. Yet for all this beauty she did not want to be a bird.

For a little while she was happy with the squirrels who had their treasures, who laboured and hunted and hid. But it was without thought or plan. Memory held them too. And it was the same with the other hoarders of the woods, the mice and voles. They seemed to be busy, but it was a business of the paws and teeth, not of the mind.

Now it was autumn again. Memory took the bears to a long sleep, whitened the hares and foxes. It was time to go back to Gauk's cave in Withered Wood, the only home she had. Yet a reluctance held her. She was not entranced by, or did not identify with Gauk's treasure, as she had with Uggi's. Nor was she utterly certain of her welcome. The dumb unicorns grazed, heavy–headed under the dropping golden birch boughs; she rode for a time on the back of one of them, the tatters of her short golden dress bright as birch leaves on its white shoulders. She wished she could see Steinvor the Valkyrie; perhaps now she might go with her.

The unicorn suddenly whinnied and shied, almost threw her; she held on to its mane, spoke to it gently, then listened. She could hear voices, smell smoke in the air. The unicorn was trembling; she edged it in under an oak, threw up her hands to a branch and climbed, squirrel fashion, while it cantered off, its horn held low.

From a high branch of the oak she could see across rough ground and scrub to where twenty or thirty men were sitting round a campfire. To one side of them were some frightened cattle, throwing up their heads and bellowing, but guarded by a few mounted men who rode round, hitting them across the eyes if they tried to move away. And, as well as these, there were three women, tied as she herself had once been, and little enough chance of any dragon coming to their rescue. She clung to her oak bough, very still, watching, and saw the men get to their feet and run to where spears and axes were stacked, and snatch them up, before she realized that another set of men had come over the ridge of heathland and were fanning out, about to attack.

She watched them fight, hoping that as many as possible would be killed, while the cattle scattered and the women screamed and tugged at their bonds. The sun that had glinted on lifted axe and shield–rim now clouded over, and through a thunderclap a Valkyrie's horse came leaping. He hovered by the oak tree; Steinvor glanced over and leant down easily towards Halla, her hands loose on the rein. "Watch me get him!" she said. Then she circled round the battle, gave one shaking yell, clapped in her heels and shot down. Leaning out of the saddle she gripped a man in mid–fall and yanked him up on to the horse. His head fell back on one side, blood splashing out of a great gash in the throat; the horse flapped back towards Halla's oak tree. She looked at the dead man and saw with satisfaction that it was her hero, the son of the King of the Dales. She hoped the wound had hurt him before he died.

"That was a neat one," boasted Steinvor, flushed, her red hair a little untidy. "I got him before he was down, even! All–Father's going to promote me Sergeant!"

"He's wearing things from our treasure!" cried Halla suddenly, her throat tightened and heart bumping.

"D'you want them?" asked Steinvor.

"Of course!" said Halla. "They're ours."

"Take the lot," said Steinvor, "he can have plenty more in Valhalla."

"Can he?" said Halla. "How?"

"Oh, All–Father hands them out after meals. Not real ones, of course. But he's not to know that. Just like they aren't real meals. Or real girls. But none of them know any better. Or ever will. Here, take the lot." She pulled the bracelets off one arm and then off the other and handed them over; the dead arms flopped back. Halla stuck the bracelets carefully on to a small branch.

"D'you want the collar?" asked Steinvor. "It's all over blood."

"It's only human blood," said Halla scornfully. "Give it to me!" Yes, it was as she had thought. This had been the pride of Uggi's famous collection of golden collars with wolf–head ends; it had shone and twinkled in a moss–lined niche at the back of the cave. Now she would clean it and polish it again. "And the rings," she added.

The horse was getting restless; his load made hovering awkward. But Steinvor duly stripped off the rings and chucked them over, sticky as they were with hero's blood. "Mucky little dragon's brat you are!" she said, and wiped her fingers on her horse's feathers and took off back into her thundercloud.

One of the rings had fallen through the branches. *Quick, quick, I must get it*, thought Halla. She climbed down, scuffled like a squirrel among the loose leaves, caught the glimpse of gold, pounced and had it, and raced back into the branches, tearing more jags in her bright, tattered dress. Safe on her branch she stared at the gold, then back at the battle which was almost over. The attackers had won, had chased off the Dales' men and loosed their own women; now they were rounding up the cattle. In the end they went off over the ridge, leaving Halla to climb down carefully, at last with the beginnings of a treasure of her own.

What now? Would she go back to Gauk and his cave in Withered Wood, which was undoubtedly a safe one? Could she bear to share her earnings? She was scrubbing her treasure now with moss and oak leaves, cleaning it up until there was no trace or smell of human blood. No, no, she could never share it, not now that Uggi was dead. It was her own, won by her own pain and fear that time, and her good sense now, paid for! And it must be hoarded up, safe, safe! Where was a cave? Where even a hollow tree, a bear's den between rocks?

She put on every bit of gold, onto herself. It was the safest way of carrying it. The sharp roundels on the collar, where it twisted over into a wolf 's head, pressed into her collarbone hollow, making her hold her head up proudly, as it was meant to do. The bracelets swung heavily, pulling her arms into awareness of gold. The hot, blinking ringstones glowed like fresh mushrooms on the dirt of her grimy–nailed bear's paws. She must hurry, hurry, find herself a cave, pile in her treasure and guard it!

Suddenly she found herself hungry for dragon's food: hot meat, spices and ginger. If she had a cave she would have all that, could waylay beasts and people. She began to run, anxiously looking for a cliff, for tumbled rocks, for a river–bed where there might be hollows. Her heart beat wildly in its own rib cave, her eyes blurred, her breath laboured, her treasure weighted her.

If only one of the unicorns would come so that she could ride on it! But no, the unicorn might want to share her treasure! Unicorns don't want treasures. But this one might. And supposing she met some of the trolls? Trolls might want anything! Trolls had eaten Uggi, might eat her, steal and throw away the gold! A giant — she hadn't seen a giant for months, years perhaps, but wasn't that all the more reason that one might come now? — might step on her, break her bracelets! Or the dwarves — if the dwarves were to see the glitter of gold — they were afraid of dragons, but would they be afraid of her? If she found a cave, how was she to know that it was not the entrance to one of the dwarves' goldmines? They might come when she was asleep, oh she must never sleep now, must watch, must guard!

PART TWO

6.

THE WANDERER

t was evening now and a light frost, crisping the fallen leaves, hardened earth and moss. And still no cave, no shelter. Before, she had not cared. She had snuggled in with the bears, in the fern litter of the foxes' den or warm between two reindeer calves. But now the forest seemed empty. She stumbled and sobbed, over–laden; the golden collar jagged at her neck. It was beginning to get dark.

She had almost touched it before she checked herself: the stiff cloak, night blue: over it the felt, wide–brimmed hat, shading the single eye, well–known disguise of One only, and so no disguise. She cowered in the leaves; of all she had feared, had she forgotten to fear this? Yet how had she come on to the path of the Wanderer? Such things did not happen unless they were intended.

"Let us sit down, my child," said the Wanderer amicably, pointing to a fallen mossy log. She did not dare, yet, to raise her eyes to his, but there was something about his voice that reminded her, sadly but also soothingly, of old Uggi. She sat, and realised that this log lay almost across the mouth of just such a cave as she had been looking for, a small, dry, cosy cave, safely beferned with niches for the holding of treasure. Longing for it she shivered and felt a fold of All–Father's cloak laid warmly round her shoulders, smelt in the dusk food laid in her lap but could not tell its nature, only that it must be good. "Eat then," said All–Father. And she ate, mousily, every crumb, licking her fingers quietly. It was food neither of dragons, nor of bears, but yet was what she wanted.

"Only the lightly burdened come to Micklegard," said All–Father, "it is a far road."

She dared to raise her eyes a little now, first to the hand that held the cloak over the knee, and sure enough it was the hand of a hero, a sword–gripper and spear–caster; but also it was a bear's paw and a dragon's claw. And as she looked at it longer, it seemed to sprout with feathers, to harden into a hoof, to be fit for all uses of nature. There was no ring on finger nor bracelet on wrist. "Shall I come to Micklegard, All–Father?" whispered Halla.

"Those who live in caves, die in caves," said All–Father, "and the love of the Wanderer is to wanderers."

Halla lifted her eyes higher until she could almost see through the oncoming darkness the face, the mouth which All–Father had shaped to speak words of kindness and wisdom to his children, the eye which he had formed to look upon them with, the shape with which he covered himself so that they might not fear him. And then she said so low that she could scarcely know if she had spoken, "It is better to have the love of the Wanderer than to be a dragon." And then one hand of hers began to pull from the other rings that were on it, and drop them onto the ground, and light, light her arms when the weight of gold was off them, and soft the stroking of chin on shoulder when the collar dropped from her neck.

In a while the Wanderer took the gold that had been her treasure and laid it in the cave, and with one hand he moved a great rock to stand in the cave–mouth, and drew down over it a great tangle of thorned bramble and blackthorn, and it was as though no cave had ever been. Then the Wanderer laid his left hand over his eye and lifted his right hand. Down onto it out of the dark wood flew the raven of foresight and spoke in his ear. When that was done he said, "For seven times seven generations of mankind will the rock stay over the cave, and then shall come what will come and, according to how the gold is used, there shall be helping or harm, making of peace or letting of blood." And he turned and gathered his cloak about him. "Travel light, my child, as the Wanderer travels light, and his love will be with you."

And then he lifted her in his two hands and set her on the back of a unicorn and he cut a fold from his night–blue cloak and laid it over her shoulders, and her fist gripped on the mane and the beast moved with her into the frosty night.

But she stayed warm and dazed and steady on its back, travelling light, with no knowledge of how she would get to wherever she was going to, nor of what she wanted to do there. And the unicorn went swiftly as the thought of the Wanderer through forests and swamps. She was aware of the passing of endless trees and cliffs under the swinging moon and once she saw without dismay that the unicorn was swimming steadily over a great waste of waters and no land in sight. Sometimes for a moment there would be faint lights from halls and houses and then again darkness. And when morning came Halla knew she had gone endlessly far from the lands she had lived in, as those may who travel light, and she was not certain at all whether this was truly the next morning after the evening in which she had met the Wanderer, or whether it was some quite other morning.

Now the place where she was seemed to be a great expanse of high and waving rushes, and in the dawn there were geese flighting and cranes. The unicorn was away, but in front of her was a small secret path through the rushes, and at the end of it thick, slow–flowing water and a light boat made out of hides stretched over a willow frame. She stepped into it and it came loose from the bank, and in a moment was floating and rocking down the current. There was a paddle in the boat, and it took her a long time to learn, first, to move in the boat without capsizing it, and then to use the paddle. By that time it was full morning, whether of the same day or some other, and this muddy, twisting channel of hers had joined with others and all together were making a wide, slow river.

In a fold of the cloak was food; there was water to hand. Day and night she drifted and slept. Her mind was clear, not more than a little sad or lonely. She was neither dragon nor bear. Once there had been a dragon's claw, hard and sharp, hidden between her breasts. It had dropped from her somewhere, on land or water. But that was not the way to remember Uggi; she wept for him a little in the early mornings, in mist and soft rain. But the sun, drying the rain off her cloak, also dried her tears. As her fingers trailed in the water the earth of the forest washed out of skin and nails. She remembered that once she had a treasure, but she did not long for it any more. She trusted in the Wanderer.

The river, low — spreading, winding between marshes or sandy bluffs, skimmed over by birds, ringed by fishes — seemed to go first towards the rising sun, then towards the noon sun, which became daily hotter and higher. In clearings of tilled land there would be huts, and nearby herded cattle, and boats with nets for the river fishing, from which men would wave and shout to the small boat. And Halla had neither fear nor hate of them, for it seemed to her they were going about the business of being people, peaceably, with no great desires nor greater burdens than they could lift. And she knew their speech, whether by virtue of dragon's blood or the Wanderer's cloak. She steered her coracle by its paddle in to land at one place or another, and she was given food and got news of crops and cattle, of life and death, and in turn took the news on to the next settlement and was welcome. Men and women would be working all day, but in the evenings they danced in rounds and sang so that their voices came clear and sad over the river.

And so in time she drifted down the Dnieper to Kiev on the high bluff and curve of the river. In Kiev there were riches and a prince; there were horsemen and pride of gold and jewels, and a market. This virtue was in the Wanderer's cloak, that folk trusted Halla and, because they trusted, were kind. So it was that a company of merchants, going to Micklegard, in a wide ship with sails and rowers, said to her that she should come with them. In return she could wash and mend and polish, and when, besides that, she did the small tricks of magic which she still remembered, they thought themselves well served and they thought, too, that Halla was under the hand of some god. As they were a company who had come together and made their merchant agreements at Kiev, their gods were various, and there were many several ways of luck and worship in which they hoped to bring themselves fortune and safety.

Halla listened to them speaking of Micklegard, and some had been there and some not. But it seemed that in the middle of that city there was a palace in which you might go from one hall into another all through a summer day and never come back again to the one from which you had started. And in these halls there was every imaginable thing. There were golden birds set with jewels that by some art opened their wings and sang. There were rare foods and delicious scents, strange animals held by golden chains, lamps that turned night into day. And in the innermost hall was the Purple–born, and on orders of the Purple–born was all done: by his word was feasting, was dancing, was racing with chariots or fighting of wild beasts or honey–sweet moving of smooth–smiling women. So this, thought Halla, sitting among hounds and hawks on the deck of the ship, listening, was the Master Dragon of Micklegard. And indeed things were believed of the Purple–born that could not be believed of any man, and nothing was too strange but that it might happen within the bounds of that place they were faring to.

As they sailed on down the river between steep brown banks, Halla spoke to the hounds, that mostly mourned for masters who had sold them, cruel though they might have been, and longed to stretch themselves in running and feel in their nostrils the scent of the nearing and fear–struck quarry. She spoke to a great hooded falcon from the north, that still in its darkened eyes saw, beyond the edges of bird–busy forest, the far crests and snow peaks and an occasional spire of dragons' breath. She spoke to horses, bred and trained for racing, that hated the sea and their captivity, the stained, evil–scented food and tainted water, horses that kicked and bit when they could. All these were merchandise going south, and so were the chained slaves, but Halla was afraid of them and they did not trust her. She said to all the animals that they would serve new and kinder masters and maybe see the Master Dragon of Micklegard, the Purple–born itself, and that they would be able to use their limbs and powers and satisfy themselves. And if the beasts were ill or hurt they would tell her, and often she could help them.

They had passed out of the mouth of the great river. Slowly the land had dropped away, and now the sails spread, almost like the great wings of a dragon. She did not think it likely that there would be mermaids in this sea, though she kept an eye open for them at first, and knew not to trust a word that they said or sung. But none came and the ship put in at one place and another along the shores of the Black Sea, and bought and sold. The merchants made profits and were glad. At a certain place called Marob they took on board three men who came down at night secretly and bargained with the Captain for a small space to lay down their cloaks and bundles. These men were anxious and afraid and yet they seemed to be good men. Only one of them could speak Greek, and that not well. But Halla, for whom all tongues were one, spoke to them in their own and they wondered at it, and after they came on board and the boat sailed, they questioned her long, how did she speak their tongue? And then they asked her, would she stay with them in Micklegard and be, as it were, their voice when talking to the Greeks?

So Halla said yes, she would do that, why not, and she asked them, did they hope to see the Master Dragon? And they said yes, that was what they wanted. They came from a country where there were no dragons, but for all they knew this could be the right way to speak of the Purple–born. For it was to him that they needed to go, to complain of tyranny by the one he had set over them, to rule them. And if once they could come to the Purple–born to tell him about this, all would be well, for was he not the ruler appointed by God over the whole world? So after that Halla began to think he must be a man and not a dragon.

The Marob men had been sent by the whole of their people to do this. But secretly, and they knew that, when it was found out as it most likely would be, by this wicked governor, then things would go ill with their own homes and the ones they had left. And one of them whose name was Tarkan Der and who was the youngest, would sit with his chin on his hands staring out over the water and thinking of this, and thinking above all of one girl and what might be done to her if things went badly. But the other two, who were older a bit, said to him that this girl, as all of those who were left, was in God's keeping, and unless it were the will of God, none should be harmed. And was it not a sign from God that this being, who called herself Halla, had been sent to them? For either she was an angel or else it would have been an angel that taught her their speech, since she could not anyhow else have learnt it.

MEN WITHOUT TREASURE

They came at last to the city on the narrow straits that some called Byzantium or Constantinopolis, but that was the same as Halla's Micklegard. It was hot and noisy and frightening, and the three men from Marob huddled together, in an altogether new kind of fear, which they had not expected, for they were all three brave men in rather different ways. Halla stood quietly, smelling about at what were new and for the most part nasty smells. Then they consulted for a little and went up together steadily from the great harbour, Halla whispering to them what the Greeks were saying so that they were not too much despised and cheated. In a while they found themselves an upper room in the narrow street of the shoemakers that stank of tanned hide, and a small room off it for Halla Godsgift, whom they treated with great gentleness and courtesy, being afraid that, if they did not, she would fly away. They brought her a blue linen dress down to the ground, and a veil for

decency's sake, but always she went out wearing the ragged end of a dark cloak, and slept under it, and they said to one another that this was surely in some way holy, perhaps a thing that had belonged to some saint, at the least a gift of God. Tarkan Der, whose far–back grandfathers had been Corn Kings of Marob in the old days, had often tried to find out from her how all this had come about. She had said to him, "Once I loved treasure and hated men. And men were cruel to me. Now I do not see men as cruel."

"Some men are cruel," said Tarkan Der and his face screwed and twitched with pain, for he knew the Governor would not hesitate once he knew what was being done behind his back. But then he said, laying his hand timidly and reverently on the cloak, "But the gift was given to you and afterwards all was changed?"

"Yes," said Halla, "afterwards all was changed."

The people of Marob had been Christians for more than a hundred years now. But it had taken its own form, and there were things believed now in Marob that might have been believed in the days of the old saints, but were no longer believed in Byzantium. It was, for instance, believed there that God was good, and that the Emperor, who had been anointed and blessed, was, if once one could come to see him, the regent and representative on earth of God, and justice would be in him, if once he could be told what had been done in his name by the wicked Governor of Marob. And then all would be well. The Governor would be punished and

the oppressed would be succoured. The hungry
would be filled with good things, the meek would
inherit the earth. The thing was, how to get to
the Emperor, the Purple–born? In Marob in the
old days it had been simple enough for anyone,
man or woman, to come to the Corn King and
ask for help. But the Corn King had gone among
the people, touching them, had gone among their
crops and beasts. The Emperor was somewhere
inside, in his palace, and when he came out of
it there were guards and courtiers, swords and
spears and gold and purple between you and
him. It had been otherwise also with Jesus; He
had gone among the people, touching them, like
a Corn King. It would not have been too hard to
speak with Him.

Morning and night the three men prayed together
and at length in the small room where they had
slept. For a little while after that, Tarkan Der would
have a feeling that the girl, who was mostly called
Sweetfeather, was in God's hand and safer than
even in his own. But, the world soon seizing on his
again, he was uneasy in a short time. Sometimes
Halla would join them, but she did not know what
the words they were saying meant, and it was not
for them to tell her. The older men, Roddin, and
Kiot, grandson of Niar, who had been a martyr in
the days of the first Marob Christians, thought
that, in her own time, she would reveal herself;
meanwhile she went with Roddin to interpret, not
only for their daily food, but when they tried to
find the way to the Purple–born.

But it seemed, beyond all, difficult to see the

one they had to see. It had appeared to them, in their innocence, that they would be able to tell a priest of what wickedness was being done in the name of the Emperor. They had been to the great church, where God and His saints and His many four–winged angels and archangels stretch overhead across the gold–glittering dome, terrible like doom, like thunder, beautiful like blessing, like the risen sun, like justice. Here surely they would find what they were seeking. They spoke the truth, humbly, in God's name, Halla saying it after them, without much thought but in Greek, so that they were understood. They were taken before a higher one, whose robes were embroidered with a wonderful glory of standing saints. One came and wrote with a pen, on a long roll. They were told that the matter would go to a higher authority. They thought that all was well. They knelt for blessing. They went back. They waited. And still they waited. And the days passed. And the money that they had brought with them became less.

In the evening, while they were sitting sadly, not even speaking to one another, a priest came. He named himself Father John, though that might well not have been his real name. All rose and signed themselves and bowed. Halla, too, made the sign of the four winds, as a bear might make it, lifting his nose to tell him from where came the sweetest scents. All spoke together for a long time and Halla took the words from one man to another. They lighted the lamp, which gave a little light but not enough to see the face of Father John and know whether or not he was speaking truth. And it was terrible for the men of Marob to need to think this of a priest, but after being in Micklegard for even as long as this, they found themselves having to.

Outside in the street of the shoemakers there was singing and some kind of tinkling instrument that was played in the dusk; after a time this stopped and they could hear that the shoemaker in the shop across the street, who never took his shutters down till late in the morning, was working still. Far off there was a scream and sounds of street fighting, then nothing much. The moon had risen and was shining through the broken corner of the shutter, seeming brighter and more silver than the lamp.

After a time all seemed to be said that could be said, and yet they did not know how this Father John had taken it. They did not know if he had been touched by the thought of justice and Christian brotherhood or even by the thought of compassion.

They looked at one another. Halla looked at a mouse that had come out in the quietness and now sat back, combing its ears with its small claws. Then with a small rustle that yet frightened the mouse away, Father John got up and went quietly down the stairs on the dark side where the moonlight could not show him to anyone who might have been watching.

"What do you make of it, Roddin?" said Kiot, running his fingers through his beard.

"If only I knew!" said Roddin. "In this place — one

can never see from one end of a street to the other, let alone men's hearts."

"It should have been easy: among Christians. But things are otherwise. It seems to me that it is as though we had come into marshes full of secret roads, and if we take a wrong step we shall drown in deep mud. We and our people."

"We cannot stand still!" said Tarkan Der. "The money is going. And so is time. And at home — at home—" Roddin put a hand on his arm. "We may need to risk taking the wrong step. None of us wants to be here one day longer than we need. I have my wife and the four children. Remember, Tarkan."

"They would not dare — with you," said Tarkan Der. "But Sweetfeather, it is not as though her father were powerful—" There was a terrible pain in his voice; it reminded Halla of a wound hurt; she wanted suddenly to lick the hurt place with a soft warm, bear's tongue, to lick it clean and into a shape of healing. But there was no wound on him that could be seen, nothing she could do but lay a hand on his shoulder, uncertainly. He put up his own two hands and gripped hard for a moment on hers, and fear came choking up in her as he did it, fear because for a moment he had seemed to her like a hero, and her hand went still as a woodcock chick hiding among leaves at a step coming.

Yet gently he loosed her and she knew it was only his wound speaking to the scar of her own. And she settled back and listened to them talking about the people of Micklegard. Roddin said, "I see it this way. Whether the Emperor knows of it or not, and God help me, I cannot be sure if he does or does not know, the Governor is protected by this high up one that Father John told us of, the one who has got the by–name Iron Gate. It is likely that some part of what the Governor, in his injustice, takes from us, goes into the hand of Iron Gate. And Iron Gate buys land and he buys men."

"And he buys the favour of the Purple–born," said Kiot sadly.

"This is what we need to think now. Having heard. And the first priest to whom we talked will do nothing against Iron Gate. And it is only by luck that the thing has not gotten to Iron Gate, and through him to the Governor."

"Not by luck," said Kiot, "but by grace. The innocent shall not always suffer."

"That is true," said Roddin. "But the scribe that wrote it down knew that there were those that hated Iron Gate, of whom one is Alexius Argyris. And Father John is his man. So the scribe said to Father John that he had something to tell him if he got his price, and by luck Father John had the money and gave it to him."

"Not by luck," said Kiot again, but this time Roddin did not seem to hear.

He went on, "Father John only chooses to help us because we might be the means of bringing down Iron Gate. He does not love us. He is not thinking about justice. That is true!" he half shouted.

"I see it that way," said Tarkan Der.

"Perhaps it is only half true?" said Kiot. But the other two, who loved him, thought all the same that he was wrong.

"So it is a question," said Roddin, "of how it will be thought we may be used as part of their design. And we must submit to be that if the Governor is to go."

"We should have given some money to Father John!" said Tarkan Der suddenly.

The others looked shocked. "But still, he is a priest of God!" said Kiot.

"I am not sure. I am not sure that what they call God here is at all the same as God."

"He must have been consecrated."

"By one like himself!"

"But it goes back — back to Saint Peter. There can be no flaw in the river of blessing. My grandfather said so," Kiot was saying this, his face anxious and troubled.

But Tarkan Der answered, "I begin to think things are different now. Can milk stay good that is left too long in the bowl, however good the cow it comes from? But it remains that we must think, how can he use us? And then we must try to use him. If nobody here cares for justice it is the only way we have—"

"I do not think that is altogether so. But the justice must look well. From their side. I think the Argyris might be the means of our getting before the Purple–born. And perhaps the only means."

Tarkan Der said, "If we give the money to Father John as a thank–offering towards the care of his poor, there is a way out for God. If he is truly a priest as we see it, then the money will go to the poor but his heart will be turned towards us. If he is not, then he will take it for himself, but we shall have bought his good will."

"How shall we know which way it goes?" said Kiot anxiously.

"We shall never know. That is part of the puzzle. Or not until afterwards. How much can we give him?"

They took from within their locked box certain gold; each man had gold or jewels sewn into his belt or his boots. And each knew what the others had. They showed it without caution to one another and to Halla, and that was strange. For there was no dragon in the world of dragons but kept back something when showing his treasure to another dragon. Indeed, they seldom showed more than a small part. All except old Uggi who had shown her everything. Because she was part of his treasure in his thought.

But these ones were saying goodbye to their treasure and they did not seem to care for it except in so far as it might get them this justice that they wanted. And it was so little a treasure. All would go on to one shelf of moss and be lost there! For a moment she felt her own love for Uggi and with it her dragonhood coming up into her eyes and on to her tongue. "You cannot give your treasure!" she said suddenly. "You must not! It is too little!"

"Is it too little?" they asked. For it seemed to them that she must have knowledge.

"Yes, yes!" she said. "A little, little treasure — keep it! Wait — if it was bigger—"

"It is all we have," said Roddin.

"It must — must be bigger—"

"I can work," said Tarkan Der. "I can go to the docks." For he had thought of that already.

"No, it is not that—" said Halla. She could not put it into words.

"We could bet on the races, then!" said Tarkan Der, a little bitterly, his voice shaken. The two older men were staring intently at Halla Godsgift. They had been once to the chariot races, in the cheapest seats, and had taken Halla. She had not at first understood about betting, but she was very much interested in the horses and trying all the time to hear what they were up to; she could hear the sound of them neighing above the muddled sound of people. One was a horse she had known on the voyage and sometimes helped. He complained that his driver was pulling at him, not letting him go full out. Other horses had laughed; they were all angry and half–hating one another. That day the men, who knew quite a lot about horses in their own country, and thought themselves judges, better at it than the city people anyway, had laid small bets on some of the races. Much to their surprise and annoyance they had lost every time. It came back into Halla's mind.

"Yes," she said. "You could do that. But first I must talk to the horses."

8.

THE HORSE'S MOUTH

alla knew her way to the racing stables by the Hippodrome. She had talked to any intelligent–looking horses while she was in the city, and also on the days when the men had gone out and left her at home, to the kites which came down on to the roof and were more knowing than the birds of the deep forest, but smelt worse.

The ones that knew their way best about Micklegard were the rats, all the same. They enjoyed the city, more perhaps than most of the men and women in it, and they knew all the little paths about it, on all levels from drains to rooftops. Especially they knew their way to all the stables, and how to get at the corn. Halla never threw stones at the rats. They were no worse than the others. She said this to the men, who saw in it a sign from God to whom all life is blessed. But they threw stones all the same. The rats never came into the room when the men were there unless they were asleep. But they knew Halla. They knew Halla was friendly to rats. When she asked them a way they told her or showed her. Why not?

The racing stables were big yards with stalls off them; the grooms slept with the horses. The charioteers, who were mostly little men with quick tempers, lived in the upper rooms. They quarrelled and sulked and sometimes poisoned one another out of jealousy. If this was found out, the one who had done it had his head held down on the shoeing anvil and his brains knocked out with a hammer; they were mostly slaves. But they went on doing it all the same.

Nobody paid any attention to Halla. She leant against the wall and talked to the Scythian horses who had come with her in the boat. One of them was terribly upset; he had eaten something which had made him ill: the charioteers were always giving queer concoctions to the racehorses which they thought would make them go faster, birds' blood and feathers for instance, and hot spices. Now this horse, who had been named in Greek, Day–Star, wanted to be quiet and eat nothing for a while and then, when he was better, to eat good grass torn by his own teeth in the field where it grew. But instead his charioteer had forced him to eat something loathsome to horses, the grooms had held his nostrils and shoved the thing down his gasping throat — he shivered all over remembering it. And then they had burnt him here and there with a red–hot iron. They had done this to drive out evil spirits which they thought had made the horse ill and had probably been put into him by a rival. One of the grooms shouted to Halla to stand back; this horse would kick her. But Day–Star was nuzzling against her, and she stroked under his chin and round his ears, saying she would try to tell the grooms. One of them came up with a bucket, and Day–Star, thinking this was some other filthy thing they wanted to force down him, kicked the groom and broke his arm.

The rest came running up and the charioteer with them. The little charioteer was yelling that he was not going to race with a vicious brute like that, and the rest saying he still had the devils in him and running to heat the irons and crack his big hide whips. And Day–Star himself yelled his hate of them all, neighing and striking with his hooves, and the men shouted to Halla to get back quick. But Halla called to them that she would quiet Day–Star if they would let her do what she wanted. So when Day–Star stopped struggling she untied his halter and led him out and gave him a drink of fresh water and praised and petted him. The others stood round at a distance. She told them that if they would not hurt him any more nor make him eat filth, Day–Star would be good.

The charioteer came over very cautiously. He looked at Halla and he looked at Day–Star. Halla said, "Look close. There are no devils in him."

"How did you do it?" whispered the charioteer. "Are you a witch? How much do you want for it?"

"I want that you should be good to Day–Star when he is good. Show him that you mean him no harm."

After a moment the charioteer came up and held out his bare hands to Day–Star who blew at them and smelt them. The charioteer lifted his hand slowly and began to stroke Day–Star's cheeks and neck. They looked at one another in the eyes. The charioteer took a ripe pear out of the fold of his tunic and held it out. Day–Star reached his head forward a little and nibbled at it. Then the charioteer ate a bit, then Day–Star finished it. "He is the best horse I have driven," said the charioteer, "but I was never sure of him."

"Why did you pull him back at the races last week?" asked Halla.

The charioteer looked round. "You know too much," he said. "You are certainly a witch!" Halla said nothing; she was not even quite sure what he meant. "No," he said suddenly. "You are not a witch! I am sorry I said it. But there are things it is best not to say, even if the saints tell one. I will not have to pull Day–Star tomorrow. But will he do the best that is in him?"

"He will do his best if you promise not to give him wrong foods nor to hurt him with whips and irons."

"It was all for his good," said the charioteer, and then, his voice shaken a bit, "I meant it, at least, all for his good."

"He did not think so," said Halla. "Do you promise?"

"Yes, lady," said the charioteer, and put his hand on his heart and bowed, for now he thought that Halla had come at least from his patron saint, and he supposed his mother had been burning candles in his name to the saint, as she sometimes did before a race, and he made up his mind that he would never laugh at her again for doing this. Secretly he said over all the prayers he could remember, and while he did this Halla spoke to Day–Star about the race. Now Day–Star really loved racing and he liked the smell and voice of the little charioteer, but he said that there was a certain groom whose smell he hated, and if he was to do his best, that groom was not to come near him. All the horses hated this man. He told her which one it was and Halla told the charioteer. As this charioteer was a freedman and well paid, and the groom was a slave and not valuable at all, it was easy to have him beaten where Day–Star could see it and taken out to be sold. Day–Star trembled and whinnied with hate and pleasure, seeing his enemy punished, and so did all the other horses, but Halla did not like it somehow.

She asked which horses would be racing against Day–Star and the charioteer told her. He wanted now to tell her everything. He was light–boned and no taller than Halla and he bowed his head over his clasped hands while he spoke to her. She went and talked to all the other horses and got them to agree that Day–Star should win and that they should tell this to the horses from any other of the stables who might be in the same race. Some of them were difficult about it, for they too loved racing; they loved to prance and show off, bouncing the light gilt chariots with the blue or green tunicked charioteers, and their own bodies brushed and combed and glowing so that every hair felt in place and every muscle ready to burst into action. Halla persuaded them that it would work out well for everyone if Day–Star were to win this race; the next race it could be another. The horses said that this might be, but the charioteers drove the chariots across one another and lashed at one another's eyes, and accidents could happen. Yet they could see that it might be best if they had decided among themselves who was to win. And for this time it should be Day–Star.

Halla was afraid they might have forgotten the next morning, but still it was worth trying. So she told Roddin to bet on Day–Star and to bet most of the money they had, and would he buy her a seat for herself close to the starting point. Now they were anxious about this and uncertain whether to take her advice, for how would she know? But at last they put heavy bets on Day–Star and bought her the seat. But for themselves, they said they would wait outside, for, if this were to work out, they would not need even to see it, and if it did not work out they would not want to have spent any of the little money they now had left on even the cheapest seats.

Halla got to her place early. In the middle of the audience there was a block of seats raised above the rest, with gilt railings and a silk awning, and in the very best place a wide and soft seat scattered with cushions of gold–embroidered leather, filled with down, and after a time the Emperor came and sat there leaning back. By now Halla had come to understand that the Purple–born was no dragon, but only a little man with thin hands and deep–set dark eyes that never seemed to look at anything and clothes that seemed too heavy and stiff for anybody to bear. He had his guards standing round him, big, tall, fair–haired men with swords and axes, long–jawed and blue–eyed. *Too like heroes*, thought Halla.

Before the chariot races there were entertainments, but many of them were cruel, showing only that some men had power over other men and over beasts. And the other men and the beasts all cried out in various kinds of fear and agony and Halla did not like it, though others, including the Purple–born, seemed to. Then there were smaller races. And at last Day–Star and the other horses, prancing and rearing, and everyone in the Hippodrome shouting and yelling for the horses and the colours they liked. Day–Star's charioteer was a green. With all that noise going on, it was easy enough for Halla to call to the horses, reminding them of what had been said, that Day–Star was to win. And the horses whinnied back, yes, yes, and she hoped they would not get too excited to remember.

In one lap of the race a tough, long–legged mare from one of the blue stables, was ahead of Day–Star for a short time. Then suddenly she dropped back — had she remembered? Day–Star was first round the winning post and Halla saw the charioteer jump down and put an arm up to pull the forelock out of Day–Star's eyes and pet him. She had also noticed that, although he had swung his whip impressively, screaming and shouting as he did so, the lash of it had never fallen on Day–Star. As they came back in triumph to the starting post he neighed at her, "I did it, I did it!" And the rest of the horses, almost as pleased with themselves as Day–Star, neighed too, "We did it, we did it!"

Halla slipped back to the others and told them to collect the winnings. She did not want to stay for anything more. So they did just that and then went to the great church to kneel and give thanks, and this they did in one of the chapels that had a small, odd–looking saint, with less rich dresses than some of them and who was perhaps not a Greek. And after that they took all the new money which they had now got and gave it to Father John for his charitable uses. Halla did not mind this much, for it was only common coined money of Byzantium, silver and a little gold and so, scarcely treasure. And they kept enough to bet on the next race. Father John thanked them gravely and said that the money would be put to the best of uses. He was anxious to know, also, whether there was more of the same kind, "for the poor," he said, and cast his eyes down, "are always with us."

Roddin said that it might be possible, but the time was going on and they were above all anxious to put their case to the Emperor. That was in hand, said Father John. So again they waited for many days and all learnt to speak the

Greek of Byzantium, though they were clumsy enough at it and would still rather that Halla should speak for them. It was odd, but Halla now found it increasingly hard, even by herself, to do the smallest bit of magic; with the others there she could not even begin.

Sometimes they went about the city, looking round them, always a little uncertain. Once Tarkan Der took Halla with him to the goldsmith's street and looked for hours at necklaces and brooches, and told her which ones he would like to get for Sweetfeather, and Halla said yes, yes, how would she wear this one or that one? And Tarkan Der talked and talked about Sweetfeather, and in his mind and fancy he was some way making up to Sweetfeather for all the danger she was in, and bedecking his own image of her in case he might seem to himself not to be valuing her enough. And yet, all the time, he knew that it was all no good, that he was no nearer to her now than at any other time, and had no more possibility of defending her real self against anything at all. So, after an hour or so, when he had chosen all the most beautiful and valuable things the goldsmiths had to show and in his fancy had given them on his knees to Sweetfeather, he turned suddenly and savagely and walked away without a word to Halla. But she was thinking there was one who would have valued the gold more than this far–off girl, and that was Uggi. He would have taken it in his claws and laid it carefully in darkness, made it part of his treasure.

9.

RATS AND KITES

hree times more, when the days of important races came round, Halla fixed with the horses who was to win, the men from Marob laid their bets, and more money went to Father John. But it was difficult because now that Day–Star had become so friendly with his charioteer, he always wanted to win. And if he was always to be the winner they would get little money by betting on him. But it was hard to explain this to Day–Star and he would not have cared; very few of the animals understood much about money. And then, what with talk by the grooms and charioteers and people putting two and two together, it began to be suspected that the men from Marob who were winning money so conspicuously at the races had something to do with the girl who hung about the racing stables and who some said was a saint or the next thing to it, and others who had lost money said was a witch.

She was talking to one of the green horses, when a rat came dashing towards her over the straw, squealing at her at the top of its voice. She paid no attention, for it did not seem right to her for rats to interrupt while she was talking to horses. The rat ran right up to them. The horse tossed his head, for he thought little of rats; and the rat stood on her foot, so that she had to notice it, but crossly. But what the rat had to tell her was that men were coming after her with sticks and stones, as though she were a rat and an enemy, and she must run for it. This fear that had never quite let her go, got her again for a moment and she could not move; she felt tied. Then the rat said, "come quick, come quick!" And he looked round at her. She followed him, running, snatching All–Father's cloak round her, not to the gate of the yard but into the corn store. He dived behind a corn chest; she had to move it a few inches, but threw a sack over the gap. And now she could hear voices — snarling, hurting, ugly voices of the hunt, the heroes out to rid the world of something they feared and hated!

At the back of the great chest she felt her way, found stones loose from the wall and crawled in, pushing herself through into dark hollows below the floor. She was wondering if the rats knew how much bigger she was than they, and horribly afraid of being caught and dragged out by the heels, backwards and helpless, her flesh crawling at the thought of that first touch. She heard footsteps above her, something banging. The place smelt ratty; she wormed her way in and along, as quietly as she could. Once she knocked accidentally into a rat's nest and someone bit her arm, but only a little. Her hair filled with rubble, her knees and elbows were scratched and bleeding. She could hear her dress tearing, but the cloak was solider stuff; she kept a bear's tooth grip on it. Then her hand, reaching out ahead, found nothing, a blank space, dark. The rat squeaked in the blackness below and a small stone dropped with a wet plop.

But she had to wriggle on; her hand reached across, found another wall and a hand–hold. She pulled herself through and dropped to where the rat had called to her, felt muck over her ankles and splashing warm up to her knees and knew she was in the stable drain. But the rats didn't care, and if they didn't why should she? Better the dung of kind horses on her feet than the grip of cruel men.

Here the rats hurried her; they could see in the dark, and they were frightened. But, for all she stooped and held her arms in front of her face, she kept on banging her head and soon she was crying as she went. The drain turned a corner, went down, the rats squeaked encouragingly, there were several of them now. She went on; by the stink of it she was in worse than horse dung here; she gasped and hurried, was cheered by the scampering rats at her side. Here and there was a shaft that let down light and fresh air; she wanted to climb out, afraid the stink would be too much for her and she would fall over into it. But still the rats hurried her, till at last she saw light ahead and staggered on, a long way it seemed, and came out below the city wall, near the sea, among rubbish and brambles. Flies swarmed. Broken pots jagged at her ankles. There was a dead animal of some kind. But the rats danced and jumped round her, whisking their tails, then scampered back into the drain. Halla went down to the sea and washed and washed, scrubbing at herself with sand, and came out in wet tatters. Then she wondered if she dared go back to the others or if the hunt was there too.

At last she saw the blunt wings of a circling kite and whistled to her. Down out of the sky she came, the handsome brown scavenger, bringing a stink of garbage with her. Halla asked her to see if there was a crowd of men near their house or any sign of trouble. The kite swung off in easy curves and Halla sat among the brambles, hoping it would be all right. The kite came back. "Many men have been there," she said, "and your men have gone."

For a moment Halla felt gladness like that of the kite soaring up, alone in her circles. No more need she be troubled for them and their treasure; no more need she be hurt by the heart–wound of Tarkan Der for Sweetfeather. Now she could be travelling light as All–Father bade her. She gave a close and bearish look about her. But this was not wild country; there was no food here for the taking, the walls of Micklegard towered behind her, watching with eyes. Behind the walls was food, but there taking was thieving, and thieving was dangerous. You needed to dive like the kite who stole meat from the butcher's stall or off the trays that the sweet sellers carried on their heads, to dive and away on wings. Feet were too slow.

Better, then, to go back behind the wall and find the men of Marob. She stood regarding the wall. Over it leaped the winged horse with Steinvor, a dead hero under her arm. The horse came down beside her, neatly planting its hoofs so as to avoid a rubbish heap, and closed its wings. "I thought it was you," said Steinvor, kicking her feet out of the stirrups, crossing one leg over the other and rearranging the hero so that he hung down tidily at each side; his skull had been knocked in, perhaps by a stone. "All–Father sent you a long way," she observed.

"I came here myself!" said Halla.

"Oh, you all think that," said Steinvor, "but we know. We're under orders. It's all there, all in the weaving. As the seed falls, so grows the tree. Look what I've got now."

"His brains are dripping out," said Halla rather disgustedly.

"He won't need them," said Steinvor. "Never did really. He was one of the Varangians, the Emperor's heroes, you've seen them."

"He made something out of it," said Halla, looking at the great golden collar that now dragged on his fallen neck.

"Oh, yes. He came here dragons'–nesting. Believing everything he was told up north. And it all worked out till this street row, when he axed a shoemaker who was trying to get the shutters up on his shop and the shoemaker's wife dropped an iron pot full of meal on his head. He'd got a new helmet and it didn't fit. If he'd stuck to his old one he'd have been all right. Serve him right, dolling himself up!"

But Halla was frowning. "A shoemaker?" she asked. "Of course. It was in your street. When the blue mob, that's Iron Gate, you know — came after you."

"But what had Iron Gate to do with the races?"

"Oh, plenty. And by that time he'd heard about your men."

"Has he killed them?" asked Halla, and suddenly, for the first time, she really hated Iron Gate. Before that he had only been a name in someone else's story. But now, if he had killed her men, it would need to be her story.

Steinvor reached over and pulled a feather out of her horse's wing and picked her teeth with it. "Oh, no," she said. "The other one got hold of them in time. The Argyris. Father John told him they could spot the winners every time and he was interested. But they're in a state about you. They think you've been killed. Tarkan Der tried to get away to look for you. They've tied him up now."

"Then I must go and find them," said Halla. She did not like hearing of people being tied up.

"There's no hurry. The Argyris crowd won't hurt them. In fact, they're going to get to the Emperor now. You know, the way they wanted. So they won't need you."

"I must be their mouth."

"Oh, the old one can speak Greek well enough for all they want. Why don't you come and join us, Halla?"

"You asked me before. I don't like heroes."

"Oh, you'd get used to them. But, of course, All–Father may have other plans for you."

"All–Father has forgotten all about me. I was only a small fly stuck in a web in a wood. He pulled me out and let me fly away."

"Perhaps. Well, I'd better take this one back or they'll wonder what's keeping me. If you want to find the Marob men, go through that gate and on until you come to the small fruit market. Then you can ask."

"Yes, there are sure to be some rats in the fruit market."

"You could even ask one of the vegetable women; you look like a little village wench. And smell like one. Comes of consorting with rats. Worse than dragons, they are."

"Do I smell?" said Halla, looking worriedly at the tears in her dress. She had washed the worst of the dirt out of it and now it had damp patches and salt stains everywhere. And the smell stuck.

"Yes, my dear! I tell you what you can do. Take this man's cloak and it'll cover everything."

But Halla stepped back. "It did me no good before, taking dead hero's gold." For she felt a dragonish twinge towards the gold fringes and clasps of the cloak and did not want it in herself just now.

"Oh, well. As you like. I must be off." Steinvor

sat back in the saddle and jerked at the reins. The horse opened one wing, then the other, and took off over the sea. Halla wrapped All–Father's cloak over the dress; the dirt seemed to have washed better out of it, and even the smell. She went through the gate, her head down, the cloak folds held tightly. She got to the fruit market and had no trouble at all in spotting a rat climbing about among the half rotten fruit chucked into the main gutter of the market, and everyone was too busy shouting how good and cheap their fruit was, or shouting back that it was bad and dear, so that they never noticed her asking her way and the rat running ahead a moment into the crooked, narrow side street with the little shops that led into another narrow and empty street, this time between high walls with trees and creepers hanging over them. And so she came to the side door of the great house of Alexius Argyris, that spread across the whole angle between this quarter and the next.

There in a small room, sitting unhappily on a bench, were the men of Marob, and Tarkan Der had his hands tied behind him and his face marked with tears. A guard was sitting on a stool, eating sunflower seeds and humming a tune to himself. Tarkan Der cried out as Halla Godsgift came in and the other two ran to her and kissed her. She asked the guard to untie Tarkan Der. "No fear," he said, "he'd knock me down if I did, the bastard. That's what he did before."

"He wouldn't now," said Halla. "He only wanted me, and here I am." So after a bit of grumbling the man untied Tarkan Der, and they all sat down again and went on waiting. By and by the guard gave them some of his sunflower seeds.

THE MASTER DRAGON

ather John came in and seemed more than delighted to see Halla, but shocked at her clothes. He had a new dress sent for and put upon her, but took great care not to touch her cloak.

Then he took them through to the inner court where the Lord Alexius Argyris was sitting on a marble seat between bushes sweet and dark with roses. There was a pool beside him with fishes; sometimes he crumbled white bread for the fishes and sometimes for a crowd of doves that jostled and swore at one another in furious dove language under the rose bushes and in the air.

He looked at the three men and Halla as though they were another kind of animal, and spoke to Father John about them as though they could not understand. Father John bowed continuously, but the others had only bowed on coming in. Part of what they said was very difficult to understand, because it dealt with people and arrangements about which not even Roddin knew anything, and Halla did not care.

At last he said to Father John, "Ask her about the races." And Father John said to Halla that His Excellence wished to know, if it was not sinful to ask such a thing, how she could tell the winner of a race.

"I ask the horses," said Halla, who was amusing herself by listening to the doves, whose language was so different from their looks.

Father John bowed nervously and repeated her answer. "She is mad," said the Lord Alexius, "but ask her for the next winner."

"How can I tell that till I have seen the horses themselves?" said Halla. "And perhaps they wouldn't do what they say. Sometimes the charioteers pull them back and stop them from winning. You ought to ask the charioteers to stop that, Lord," she added. "It spoils the races for the horses."

Lord Alexius laughed. "Perhaps she is not so mad after all. What do you think of her, Foxy?" For this was the shocking name which he used to the priest of God, Father John.

Father John drew himself up and said, "Her madness is from on high." And he signed himself.

So did the three men from Marob, and in time, Lord Alexius, but lazily and flourishing the rings on his fingers. He looked at them again and turned to Father John. "You think their story will stand?" Father John nodded. "Then tell them they are to go to the Palace tomorrow. And feed them," he added, "and let them remember who has helped them. Later on I shall make the girl talk to the horses. That will be something new."

He turned his back and walked out. Father John took them to a better room with carpets and hangings, and ordered slaves to bring food and wine, which was better than any they had eaten all this time, and he ordered Tarkan Der's sword, which had been taken from him, to be given back. Then he told them how, out of his Christian charity, the Lord Alexius Argyris would take them before the Emperor and they could tell their story and justice would be done and the innocent succoured. And they thanked him, but Roddin felt in his heart that he was not as glad about this as he would have been at the beginning. Nor yet as certain what would come of it. Nor yet even as certain that, supposing things worked out well, it would be for any kind of right reason.

Father John pressed them to eat, and especially to drink, more, and carefully tried to get Halla to tell exactly what she did about the races. Halla made no mystery about talking to the horses, but she did not want to tell about her difficulties with Day–Star, in case they might try to separate him and his charioteer. She felt that this was just the kind of thing which might be done here. Anyhow, Father John did not believe her; he could not believe in anything so simple. But perhaps the Marob men did. After he had gone she told them how she had escaped through the drain, but did not say that the rats had helped her. It was queer, but most people disliked rats, although in so many ways rats behaved the same. "We were afraid they had killed you," said Roddin, "for all you are protected. But they come between God and His ways and will, in this place."

"For all their churches," said Tarkan Der. "Even the bricks have rottenness in them. A man told me you were killed, and for a little while I did not believe in God. And I did not forgive my enemies."

"God help us," said Kiot, "I wish we were out of here."

"And the thing done we are here for," said Roddin. "Sometimes I wonder — if we had known how it would be—"

"How long," said Tarkan Der, "and no news."

"You will go back to her, son," said Roddin."If there is danger, she will be hidden. You know how many friends you have."

"If there is any kind of warning," said Tarkan Der, "but if they come at night — and take her away — O God!"

"Let us pray," said Kiot, "that this cup pass from you and from all of us." So they knelt and prayed. Halla knelt with them and thought of Steinvor, and the rats, and the cleverness and beauty of the swooping kite.

The next day a big covered litter, carried by eight men with two spares, was brought into the courtyard, and the three men and Halla told to get into it. Then the curtains were drawn; they felt themselves lifted, jolted, moving. Tarkan Der tried to see out through a chink, but a hand outside pulled the curtains sharply together. Inside the litter it got very hot. The men of Marob in their thick clothes sweated and worried. Tarkan Der killed all the flies, one after the other. Halla watched him; she had no great feeling for flies; you could not want to share any of their qualities. Roddin stuck his fingers through his beard. "When we get to the Emperor," he said, "the first thing is to make certain that he knows we are sent by all the people of Marob, not only ourselves."

"The first thing," said Tarkan Der bitterly, "is to remember all Father John told us about bowing and kissing the floor and behaving like animals."

"No animal kisses the floor," said Halla, "it is only men." Tarkan Der laughed and put his arm round her. She did not mind. They were all glad he was laughing.

Kiot said, "We do not know what will have been said about us. Anything may have been said. It will all have been mixed up with this street fight. The Emperor is bound to have been told about that, at least, with his guards being in it."

"I spoke a little with one of them," said Tarkan Der. "He says he is going away from here soon. He is going to another city called Holmgard, as soon as he has treasure enough here."

So there were some who did get treasure, Halla thought. But was he a hero or did he mean it to be true treasure — dragon treasure? Had he a cave in his mind? "Where is Holmgard?" said Roddin.

"North. North. Beyond where we are. Beyond the Red Riders. He said there is snow there for five months in the year. There is another name for it; the folk there call it Novgorod. And the Emperor's law does not run there. They have a rule of their own."

"That would be good," said Roddin.

"There was a time," Kiot said, "when we believed that the Emperor's rule also meant the rule of God. It was what the first priest said. My grandfather Niar died because that was true then."

"Or because he thought it was. Certainly he died because of what he believed to be good. If we had not come here we might be believing it still."

"And now," said Tarkan Der, "now at the best we lose a bad Governor and get perhaps a good one. But we shall not be able to believe that he comes from God. The people of Marob will welcome him as the Ambassador of God. But we shall know that it is not that at all. We have become separated from the others."

"If things had gone on in the old ways," said Roddin, "you might have been Corn King of Marob, Tarkan Der."

"I might," he said. "Yes, Roddin, I have thought of that." And he dug his face down into one of the cushions of the jolting litter.

Now there was a halt and a challenge and the jangling sound of soldiers. The litter was put down, but still there was no chance of plucking the curtains apart and seeing where they were. The litter was taken up and this time they were jolted and tilted up steps, falling against one another. Then they were set down and allowed to get out. They were in a long, barrel–vaulted hall with painted sides where horsemen stiffly pranced, larger than life, red–fleshed and black–eyed; huge hunted hares galloped across spear–pointed grasses. Ahead there were curtains hanging in still folds. They looked at one another and whispered. Roddin took the bone comb out from under his belt and pulled it through the stiff grey hairs of his beard, then passed it round. Halla, jagging at the snarls in her own hair, thought there must still be plaster in it.

Father John came in, to tell them that the moment was come. And they must remember the prostration, the advance on knees only. "Let me keep your cloak," he said to Roddin, "it will be easier." And he took their heavy felt cloaks, edged, Marob fashion, with other colours of felt and shells sewn into patterns at the corners. But when he came to Halla, she stepped back, saying "No," and he did not dare to insist, for he knew when others had the thing in their spirit which he did not have himself. "Come," he said.

Beyond the curtains they went for a few steps in almost darkness, on a floor sloping up, then suddenly in light. Although outside it was a hot and cloudless morning, yet within curtains were drawn and candles blazed on an amazing glitter of colour, the solid blue of lapis, the green of malachite, the veined purple of porphyry, and everywhere gold in whatever shapes could be made out of it, tall candlesticks, door handles, small fountains, swinging lamps, scent bowls, in this lighted cave, the cave indeed of the Master Dragon, thought Halla. Father John whispered "Now — down!" And all went on their knees and advanced crawling or bowing towards the same little man in heavy robes whom Halla had seen at the races. Still his eyes did not look at anyone, but always beyond them. Kiot, also seeing this, thought sharply that not so had Jesus looked at mankind, not so the Corn Kings.

At last they were kneeling close to him on a rug woven with fabulous birds; they could see his feet in gold–sewn purple leather boots, but he was still two steps up from them on his throne. And on the first step stood the Lord Alexius Argyris with a parchment in his hand. Behind them a secretary in a long green coat braided with black was standing ready to take notes, pen in hand, inkwell at his belt.

The Purple–born muttered something; they could not catch what. But Father John, from behind, told them that they might kneel upright. It seemed that the Purple–born had asked about the woman, and it was explained that the woman was their voice and also that she was gifted in other ways. It was to be observed that she was never to be seen without the cloak fold, and this had all the appearance of being a Relic. The Purple–born showed himself interested and said that, if this was so, the cloak should be taken from her and given to one of the churches. Doubtless this was intended. The cloak might indeed go into Father John's keeping. Father

John bowed deeply. "Later," said Lord Alexius, "later, it shall certainly be done." None of them, of course, spoke, but Halla clutched on to her cloak and wondered what All–Father would say to this.

"Now let us hear what they have to say," said the Purple–born. "Tell them to speak."

The Lord Alexius signaled to Roddin, who began his speech, remembering at first all the titles which Father John had warned him he must use. He backed what he had to say with texts, from the New Testament mostly. The other two kept their eyes down. Kiot was praying. He felt that this was the way he could help best. Halla, calmly watching, saw that, while Roddin was quoting passionately from this thing which was altogether part of his life and the reason for his actions, the Purple–born was unmoved, and once yawned slightly, while the Lord Alexius had a little thin smile sneaking about his face. Father John turned up his eyes and went through the gestures of religious observance which now she thought she knew. The secretary noted the texts but did not trouble to write down the words.

Questions were addressed through the Lord Alexius. Who exactly were this deputation and what did they represent? Roddin, not having his answers by heart, stammered a little over words. Halla became his mouthpiece. How long had Marob been part of the Holy Roman Empire? And in what circumstances? They told him, and Kiot spoke of his grandfather, the martyr, and Halla put it into Greek. As he told about Niar and how he had let himself be killed because of his belief, because he felt himself to be on the side of goodness and mercy and justice, so Halla became aware of what all this was about and why these men prayed and why she felt love for them all and liked to help them and to understand their language.

The questions went on. The Purple–born crossed one boot over the other and laid his fingertips together. Sometimes he spoke in a low voice to the Lord Alexius. Twice they heard the name Iron Gate, once followed by the Lord Alexius spreading his hands and giving a sharp snickering laugh and the Purple–born raising his eyebrows and then speaking over his shoulder to the secretary.

Another question followed to gather details of what cruelty and injustice had been done by the Governor. All three spoke in answer, Halla looking from one to the other, taking the words quickly and making them into Greek. Roddin had tears in his eyes, speaking of certain things that had been done. Even the Purple–born seemed slightly disturbed. Then the Lord Alexius said, "And I have a statement from a merchant whose ship put in at this place after these men left. It tells of further tyrannies." He unrolled his parchment, and the three men, suddenly realising that this was news from home, stayed very quiet, listening.

It became a catalogue of unjust accusations, fines, imprisonments, abductions, torture and murder. Occasionally there was a name, a

Marob name, turned into Greek. But almost at once the men knew who it must be. Halla could see them stiffen and wince. Kiot's hands were locked together in a tenseness of supplication. Once, Tarkan Der's right arm lifted in the first movement of a man reaching for his sword. It went on to say that the Governor had found out that certain men of Marob had left for Byzantium, and such was his spite and cruelty that he had taken the betrothed of one of them, a girl called Sweetfeather. And certain things had been done to her until she died. Now Roddin had Tarkan Der by the shoulders, holding him. And Halla felt as she had done when Uggi came trailing back to his cave with the death wound on him, felt the terrible need to take another's pain, and no way to do it. And Tarkan Der put his hands on to the pit of his stomach and gave a horrible low choking cry as though he had got a deep wound there, and the blood left his face.

It seemed to be a very long time after that, yet it was only minutes, when the Purple–born got up from his chair and spoke to them for the first time directly. "Out of my sacred Clemency and Imperial Justice I pronounce that your Governor is dismissed and will receive punishment. The choice of his successor is in the hands of my well–trusted friend, the Lord Alexius Argyris. So you may rest assured, my children, that all will be well and that our power reaches to the ends of the Christian world!"

"Down!" whispered Father John. "Down!" And they bowed their foreheads to the carpet

until the Purple–born was away. Then the Lord
Alexius was speaking to Roddin about the new
Governor. Halla stood by them as interpreter,
since Roddin also was shaken. If this had been
done to Sweetfeather — and it was making him
sick to think of it — what might not have been
done since then to his own children and wife. He
said that he hoped they might all be allowed to
go home at once.

"Certainly you can go," said the Lord Alexius,
"in the boat which takes the new Governor and
under his favour and protection. We have been
not unaware that your gratitude for the help
received here has taken the form of gifts to the
poor. This was very suitable, yes, very suitable
indeed. But on the matter of the races," he added,
"I must question the young woman. And as the
Purple–born himself desired it, her cloak, which
is doubtless an important Relic — and she will
have to explain how she came by it and to which
saint she owes it — should remain here in the
capital of the world. Where it will be safe."

Roddin raised his head to answer and clearly
there was anger on him. But Halla caught at
his hand, whispering, "Say nothing — leave it
to me." So she gave a meek look and said that
she would be at His Lordship's service, but she
must first go back with the others and help them
to settle with their landlord and perhaps to see
whether it might not be possible to contribute
still further to the charities of the great city.
After that she would tell him everything that he
wished to know.

So he agreed and said, too, that Father John should bring them round the merchant's deposition in case there was anything in it which they had not properly understood. Then he sent for the large litter to take them all back. They got into it and it started. It was the same heat and jostling and sounds from without that there had been coming. But all was different. And now Tarkan Der, who had not yet wept, began to shake all over and deep long sobs came out of him, and his body moved jerkily like a half–killed animal. Halla moved over and sat by him and took his head on to her knee to ease his weeping.

PART THREE

11.

AWAY

hey were back in the small room. The shoemaker, who had thought them decent and quiet folk, and had been disturbed when none of them came back after the guards took them, asked what had happened. They told him that their mission had been successful, that the Emperor had seen them, but there had been bad news from home. The shoemaker, glancing from one to the other, saw that this had indeed been so.

"And the Emperor received you himself!" he said. "That was a wonder! You'll have something there to remember all your lives."

"We shall," said Roddin, but in a voice that troubled the shoemaker so much that in a little he sent his wife up with sweet wine and almonds and his respectful compliments. She wanted just desperately to ask them all about the palace and the Emperor's robes, but with them looking the way they were, she hadn't the heart.

Then Father John came to tell them that, if they cared to take the chance, they might get home even before the new Governor. There was a ship bound for Olbia which would put in at Marob if they wanted to go straight away, and it seemed to them that he would be glad to get rid of them, even as they themselves wanted to get away, from him and from Byzantium. But this ship was to sail with the morning tide next day, so they would have to get ready at once. Should they have affairs to settle, for example any small thankoffering they might care to make, he would see to it for them.

"Yes," said Roddin. "Yes. We will go."

"And she stays." Father John looked at Halla in a way which she found it difficult to make sense of, but she knew he was planning somehow to make it a certainty. To keep her here — forever.

"Yes!" she said quickly. "I stay!" And she signed with her hand behind her to the others.

Roddin said, "When is the Governor recalled?"

"One of the Imperial despatch boats will start on the same tide as yourselves, but going fast. He will be gone before you get there."

"Thank God for that. And the new one — he is a friend of the Lord Alexius Argyris?"

"And a true Christian," said Father John.

"A true Christian — then he is a poor man?"

"No, no," said Father John. "On the contrary, he is very rich. He will not need to make you pay heavy taxes." He smiled at them, even perhaps wishing them well, having a kindliness towards them in his heart, now that they had helped in his own schemes. "And he will know," said Father John, "that the Lord Alexius is your patron, so that he will certainly help you take revenge on your enemies."

"But the old Governor will be gone."

"You will certainly discover," said Father John, with the foxy, biting look on him, "that there were some of your own people as well as the late Governor who… were involved."

Tarkan Der looked up for the first time. "True enough," he said. There had been a man in the old days who had wanted Sweetfeather, but she… she. He found he could not think of her yet for more than a moment without this terrible sick feeling coming over him again.

Roddin said quickly, "You will tell the captain of this ship that we are coming. And when you return you shall help us about our affairs." Father John bowed himself out, and he gave a long sideways look at Halla, sitting on a stool in her new dress, with her hands in her lap.

Kiot said, "So this rich Christian Governor who is the creature of the Lord Alexius will help us to avenge ourselves. And later on, when there is a swing–over of power here, or when this Emperor is poisoned and another comes in his place, a new Christian Governor will come from Iron Gate and avenge others on ourselves, and so in the name of God and his Holy Roman Empire it will go on, world without end. It is as well that my grandfather cannot know what he died to give us." And now Kiot was more bitter than the other two because he had believed longest that after all Byzantium was somehow the true dwelling–

place of the doctrines of the Lord and of His regent on Earth.

Roddin said, "I am all shaken in my mind. Perhaps we should try to stop the new Governor from coming. Tarkan Der, child of the Corn Kings, will you lead the people of Marob?"

Tarkan Der looked up and shook his head. "No. Not now. I will never go back. And if I did they would send an army against us. They could pay for an army and not risk one single life of their own."

"Will you not ever come back?" said Roddin, very pitifully.

"No," said Tarkan Der, "I cannot bear to look on Marob, even. And besides that, I am very full of hate and perhaps I could not forgive my enemies. I could be led into temptation. I cannot get at the beginnings of forgiveness even. So I will go where that Varangian told me there was another place, to Holmgard in the north. It is a better city than this. Or so he said."

"What could you do there?"

"If it came to that I could be a fighter, a guard to the king there. Those I might kill that way would not be my enemies; I would have no temptation. They would only be the enemies of some king. It would not matter to me nor yet to God. But I will not go back to Marob."

"Maybe I too —" said Roddin.

"You are older than me. You can face whatever is to be faced. They need you. But they would be better without me. I might do harm to Marob. I feel it in myself. I will go with you in the ship, but when we come to Marob I will sail on with her, to Olbia and beyond. I will go alone from now on."

"Perhaps I will go to Holmgard," said Halla.

Suddenly they were all thinking of her. "Oh, Halla Godsgift, our Halla," said Kiot, "what will you do?"

"I think some way I will be on the boat," said Halla.

"How will you escape?" Roddin asked anxiously. "For we cannot leave you here. In this Godless place. We love you."

"I am not staying," said Halla, "but I do not know how."

"Go now!" said Tarkan Der.

"Father John would certainly not let you onto the ship if I did that. He has got to think he is sure of me. We must say goodbye. But I tell you I will come."

So they left it for the time to Halla and to the God who had given her to them. They packed their bundles and they agreed to give a certain amount of what they had left to Father John, who came that evening and took them down to the docks. Here Halla said goodbye to them and they were terribly unsure if they would truly see her again in this life. Sweetfeather too had been in God's hand, but God had not had it in His will to save her, and who could know what was in His will for Halla? Roddin and Kiot kissed her, and then suddenly Tarkan Der kissed her and it was a fierce, long kiss, and he had a dazed look on him afterwards. But Halla went back with Father John and he was speaking to her about the races. He was telling her of the great good that might be done, say, to a nunnery, by this gift of prediction, and perhaps she should become a nun and give not only her cloak but all her other gifts to God. Indeed, if she did not do that, it might appear that her prediction was from Satan, and that would indeed be a serious thing for her.

She had heard of nunneries and the power that some of them had and the golden vessels in their chapels, but she did not know what was the occasion of them. So she asked Father John and listened carefully, so that he thought he must be prevailing on her to take his advice. And from time to time he got the talk round to her cloak and where did it come from, but she always let this go by; and then again he would speak of her business with the horses, and how, for the greater glory of God and in order to help her friends who had gone back to their home, she should tell the Lord Alexius Argyris the way some great race was to go. And she was thinking to herself that if she angered the Lord Alexius it might do harm to the men of Marob when they got home, and she must tread carefully.

Father John then said to her that it would be better for the sake of her good name if she were to stay from now on in a nunnery, and she agreed gently, and went with him, turning over in her mind how she could possibly talk to any of the horses in front of the Lord Alexius. It was certain that they would not like him, nor trust her if she was with him. There was no knowing how Day–Star or the others would act. Well, she would see when the time came.

Father John took her and her small bundle to the nunnery. The men had wanted her to keep some of their money, but she would only take a very little. Travel light, she said to herself. She was put in charge of an elderly, tall woman, dressed all in black with a white veil, who spoke earnestly with Father John and in the end knelt for his blessing. This displeased Halla because she thought that the woman looked good. Then Father John was taken to the gate and the key turned behind him and then put back on to the girdle of the tall woman, who spoke to her kindly. Now it was late evening and still Halla could think of no way to get to the ship.

The nunnery seemed to be made up of a hall, a chapel and many smaller rooms round a courtyard; in one of these Halla left her bundle. There was supper and then all went to the chapel and prayed, taking Halla with them. And then it was night. Halla stayed awake and after everything was quiet she got up and began to go about the place cautiously. If she could find a rat or even a mouse she might yet find a way out. She felt her way in the dark into the kitchen, but there was no scuffling of little paws and all was clean and quiet. The walls were too smooth and too high to climb and every gate was locked and barred. When it was near dawn she went back to her cell and thought of the ship sailing on the morning tide and the three men waiting for her. And she wanted above everything to tear down these walls that kept her from them. But such bearishness did no good. And maybe, she thought, goodbye is goodbye and there is something else coming to me. Yet she had it strongly in her mind that she should be going on the way to Holmgard. Thinking that, she slept, and then it was day and the ship would have sailed.

She sat herself down in the courtyard and watched what was going on. Sometimes the tall woman spoke to her. In one of the larger rooms four other women, also dressed in black, were sewing in silence at robes of gold and purple. In a shadowed part of the courtyard another such woman was painting on a leaf of parchment; a little, stiff, beautiful world. But a bell sounded and immediately all left what they were doing and hurried into the chapel. They looked at Halla, but she did not follow them. Instead, she went and stared at the half–painted leaf; in the edges were looped patterns, some drawn in with fine lines and others already painted with thick colours and gold. In the very middle of the picture was a throne of gold and one sitting on the throne with a dark, purplish beard and eyes golden and black and a patterned golden glory behind his head. All–Father was not like that.

As the shadows lengthened, the nuns brought out the sick people, whom they cared for in one of the rooms. There was a charioteer who had been thrown and dragged; he had a broken leg and arm and bad cuts and bruises and he kept on crying because he was afraid he would never get back to the racing; he was unfree and he might be sold as cheap labour if he did not heal well. He was always wanting to speak about the racing, but none of the nuns who were looking after him had ever seen a race, so it was no use his trying to speak to them. But Halla talked to him and after that for a little he was quieter. The tall woman observed this with commendation in her face.

Another of these men was one of the master carpet weavers; he was sick in his stomach and groaning. And yet another that they brought out seemed too ill even to groan; he had a jagged wound in his side and although it looked not too bad from the outside, clearly there was something badly wrong within. He, they said, was a man from the Emperor's Guards, the Varangians, and he had been wounded in the street fighting two days back. He was most probably dying and they had tried to find out whether he was a Christian, but his companions who had brought him in did not know and did not appear to care. So they put a crucifix upon his chest and the struggling breath within it, and laid his hands on the crucifix, and by and by a priest came in case the man was to speak. But he did not speak in any clear words, and his breath came in worse gasps, and now his eyes were half shut with only the whites showing. Halla was watching him. He was red–haired, and even on his hands and wrists there were red thick hairs; he had a gold ring on one finger with a ruby in it.

She felt a horse blowing on her neck and turned. "It's you again!" said Steinvor. "Whatever are you doing here?"

"I don't want to be here," said Halla. "Can you take us both? And then leave me on the ship?" For she guessed Steinvor had come for the Varangian: he had all too much of a hero's looks.

"Well, seeing you're another of All–Father's wish children, I suppose I can," said Steinvor, "but you can't expect us to make good time; you aren't exactly a lightweight. Stand by till I've got a grip of him and then get on behind. And mind you hold on." She glanced at the man. "Take that cross off him, there's a good girl: it might burn my fingers."

Halla went over to the man, took the crucifix off him lightly and laid it to one side, as his chest heaved once more. Before the priest had done more than look astonished, the last breath came out of the man, and Steinvor leant over and grabbed him up by the shoulders. Halla ran and jumped and scrambled up behind onto the winged horse, holding her cloak round her with her teeth, both hands with their own grip on the horse as he rose. She shut her eyes and held as they mounted; then he steadied up and flattened and they were away over the roofs, and suddenly it was like flying with Uggi and Hroar and the rest, and she felt at ease, back in her childhood. But she hung on all the same.

The nuns and the priest, not expecting nor believing in a Valkyrie, did not see one. But they saw the dead man vanish and Halla whirled away to heaven, unfortunately still with the cloak, which no one had had the presence of mind to retain. She had, however, left her bundle in the cell. This, they agreed, must certainly be tried out as a Relic. If anything in it had miraculous powers, then something, at least, would have been gained.

12.

MAROB

he winged horse was grumbling away and obviously would have liked nothing better than to chuck her off, but Halla said the ship could not have gotten far and they circled down over the mouth of the Black Sea. There were two or three ships, looking very small, with the bright wave at their prows; Halla was not sure at first which was the right one. But then she saw Tarkan Der's yellow shirt, which was an uncommon colour, and she had washed it often enough to know. And there were the other two. She slid off on to the deck beside them from a height of some fifteen feet — nearer the horse would not go — but she landed without hurting herself. When she had picked herself up and had finished assuring them that it was indeed herself and everything was all right, the horse was far off, a speck in the northern sky, galloping back to Valhalla.

She did not explain how she had come. It would have been too difficult. They had no word or thought for a Valkyrie. She was content to be with them, in a ship again, and they were very content to have her with them whom they had thought lost. There was now no action which they could take. The ship carried them on.

Often they sat, speaking very little, for hours at a time, and the sea went by past them, deep green or deep blue. Sometime Kiot walked up and down and muttered; he had been terribly shaken; he was an oldish man and he had tried to live all his life as a Christian; he would have forgiven the Governor for anything done to himself, but it was not about that he had come; it was about injustice to the whole community which had surely been of the same kind — only worse — as that injustice of the Pharisees which Jesus had struggled against in bitter anger. He was right to come. Yet if he had not come, if he had forgiven the Governor for something which was not forgivable, then he would not have been disturbed to the roots of his being. Long ago he had heard of the great Church of the Holy Word, Santa Sophia, wonder of the Christian world. Now he had seen it, and the sight had been sore on him, since it was mixed up with certain and personal knowledge of the Church's corruption. He tried not to think of it. He tried to go back in prayer to what he had once been, but that road was shut to him. He felt an old man now, as he had not done on the voyage out.

Roddin knew what was wrong with his old friend and could not help in any way. They had done what they meant to do, but now it was not clear that it was good, and the price was yet to pay. And Tarkan Der, the heir of the Corn Kings, was not ever coming back to Marob. Roddin watched him as he sat looking out to sea, and his face seemed thinner and harder, and his hand now and then, almost on its own, reached back jerkily and grasped the hand of Halla Godsgift. Did his mind even know what his hand was doing? On the way out he had sung, often; he never sang now.

Roddin and Halla did the cooking together. Roddin had told the captain of the boat that she would be coming, and then she had come. When a sailor said she had fallen out of the sky, the captain knocked the sailor down for telling lies. Anyhow, he was not interested in where the girl had come from. She behaved decently, gave no trouble, kept a flat stone under their charcoal cooking stove and understood when she was spoken to. When they came to a port she would go ashore with one of the men and buy whatever they needed. Slowly the boat worked her way along the coast. The Imperial dispatch boat had passed them on the evening of the first day. The wind had died down and they themselves were scarcely moving, but in the despatch boat the slaves were rowing hard and evenly, like some unhuman thing.

Although he knew how useless it was to fret about an unknown situation, although he prayed often, Roddin found himself sleeping less and continually turning over in his mind how, with what words, with what armour, he could meet bad news if it came. His face would whiten and twist and go still. He was afraid of the same thing hitting him as had hit Tarkan Der. He was afraid of becoming remote from his old friends as Tarkan Der was now, in a small world of pain. He asked himself if Halla Godsgift were not now perhaps nearer to Tarkan Der than he or Kiot were.

The days went on. Once there was a storm and they were all seasick. Afterwards there were calm days and Halla talked to the porpoises that played round the ship and half thought of joining them, such delight as was in the slither, the dive upwards into warm air, the feel of dryness momentarily on the skin, light momentarily on the dazzled eyes, and then the dive downward into wet coolness and translucency. But perhaps, she thought, it would not work out that way for me. Fire I know, but water makes me think of mermaids, and so do the tails of the porpoises. And there is no dragon here to get me out of it if I make a mistake.

And then the uneasiness of the men began to increase. It all began with a low headland that came into sight, greenish, with a long sandbar that the boat stood well out from. After that they stayed all the time by the rail, watching. Or Tarkan Der turned his back on it, staring out, instead, over the enormous unbounded sea on the other side. This went on for two days, and then Roddin and Kiot began to get their bundles together. Each in turn, they tried once more to persuade Tarkan Der to come back with them. He would not come. And now they were turning inland into Marob harbour. He hid himself in under the foredeck among ropes and sails. Halla went to look for him; he had turned bearish, in a den, head buried between paws. When she spoke, kneeling beside him, he pulled her down suddenly on to the cold sail, arm heavy on her neck, his wet cheek by hers. For a time they stayed so. If he could sleep, she thought, sleep through the unhappy months, the heart's hunger, the months of death and cold and not having what you most want, and wake with time gone past and blurred and a new year coming. But perhaps it is too early in the year, she thought after that, and besides, he is not a bear.

She moved away from him gently and covered him in with a spare sail. The ship was making fast. The other two were ready to go. Halla went with them, but she said she would be back before sunset, when the ship sailed again. She had heard so much about this place of theirs. And now it was real. And now someone had seen them and known them, bent quickly to kiss their hands, hurried them up from the harbour and into a house. They had become part of it again. She followed.

They were speaking quickly and low, while Halla looked round, seeing the things in the house a little different from things in other houses: the water pot and the meal chest, the way the hearth for the fire was built, the fish–nets weighted with Marob stones, the harness for Marob oxen, the hinge on the shutter, the sneck on the door, the pattern in the weaving, all making up to another way of doing and other words for what is done. She saw Roddin's face smooth over with gladness and he turned to her, saying that his wife and children had taken refuge in time with her father, who had kept them safe. His own house had been seized by the Governor, most likely everything was gone, the horses, the furnishings — but that did not matter. Nothing mattered. And the Governor had been recalled, had gone back with the Imperial despatch boat, in anger and violence; yes, people had been killed in the last days, things destroyed. But it was known that the three who had set out for Byzantium had done what Marob wanted them to do.

More people came into the room; it was hot and darkened with them. One asked about Tarkan Der. "He is never coming back," said Roddin. Then one of them nodded and said that it was not only Sweetfeather but also Yillit had come back too soon and had been caught and killed in the last days, and also in a shocking way. Roddin turned to Halla, "That was his young brother, whom he had thought safe. He need never know what happened." And Halla nodded.

There were still friends of the old Governor about, who swore that he would come back. It would be best for Roddin and Kiot to keep hidden until the new Governor came and all was well and there could be thanksgiving. But meanwhile God could be thanked for His mercies in many hearts. Kiot looked sad and grave at this, but then another man came in. He was wearing the dress of a priest, but simple, and there was kindness in his whole look. He and Roddin and Kiot kissed one another and made the cross sign, and it seemed to Halla suddenly that those two had come back into something they needed for their life, like the porpoise diving back into its own water world.

Now some of the people had gone out of the house and now the light was beginning to glow and come shallowly into the room through the low window opening, and Halla knew she must go. She said goodbye quickly and the two men touched her face and hands and the folds of All–Father's cloak, and she went back to the harbour and aboard. The captain of the ship was getting ready to cast off, for he had a fair land wind to take him out to sea.

As they drew out of Marob harbour she went down and pulled the sail quietly away from over Tarkan Der. He looked at her and there was dust on her sandals, and he was staring at that. And she said, "I will wash it off." He gave a little nod and covered his ears against with his hands, waiting until they were well out of hearing and at last out of sight of land.

13.

FIRE

S o now they were going north again and it was getting less warm and they came to the flat delta and sandy coast, the stain of the great river flowing into the sea, and so to Olbia. It was queer, but Tarkan Der was getting better now. He could even sing a little. It was the same as the forest birds in the first days of spring, thought Halla, when the sun warmth began to soak through their cold feathers. Soon enough they were singing all days. So now he sang to himself, walking through the main street of Olbia, one arm round Halla, looking for other travellers who were going by the east way, up the river and so on to Holmgard or Novgorod or however they called it. He was doing the asking himself, would not let her help him. Their speech in Olbia was not too different from his own in Marob, and there were always some that spoke Greek. Now that he would have no more need, ever, of that, it seemed that he wanted to speak it. They came down to the quays along the side of the river. Out of the corner of her eye, Halla saw the shadowy flitting of rats over and among the heaped grain sacks. She stepped back and questioned them. Who knew better the movements of ships?

Yes, there was a river ship loading now, thirty good rat–runs away up the quay. She told Tarkan Der. "Halla Pathfinder!" he said, and suddenly took her in both arms and kissed her. She disengaged herself, uneasy about this and yet for all that so much liking Tarkan Der and wanting his good. He did not repeat it, only held her hand and sometimes swung it. When they got to the big, broad–bottomed river boat he bargained cleverly, and there was space set aside for Halla. In a short while the boat was loaded and they began to pole her out from the quayside and the dodging bright rat eyes watching them go.

Upstream they went, using what wind there was in the square, heavy sails, but with slaves at the oars all day, tugging them along against the current. Now Halla was sorry for the slaves and spoke to them in what each knew, in a dim surprise, to have been once his own tongue. But Tarkan Der looked at them being tired out and hurt, and did not care. For a time mercy was dead in him.

They came to Kiev, which she remembered. There was fighting there between two kings. A man came down to the ship and spoke to the captain and then to Tarkan Der, asking him to join in the war, promising good pay. There was wine poured and drunk. Tarkan Der was speaking in a voice that Halla, standing a little way off in the prow of the ship, had not heard on him before. At last he shouted her name and she came, and he asked her, should he go or not go and fight for the Prince of Kiev against his enemies? "What is this war?" asked Halla. The man said eagerly that it was a war against rebels who must be crushed before they became strong. "This prince," said Halla, "is he a just governor?"

The man began to speak, but Tarkan Der's face and voice had changed. "I had forgotten," he said, "but I am a Christian."

"But the Prince is a Christian," said the man. "He has built a great Church, a wonder of the world, He has founded nunneries —"

"I had forgotten," said Tarkan Der, "I have to go further, I am not landing here." And the man went away angry, swearing there would be punishment, but Tarkan Der did not care at all.

Yet the next day when they set off again, he was frowning and troubled and not speaking much. At night he asked Halla to let him sleep under the cloak, for he was not sure whether he had acted right and he needed guidance, and maybe God would send him a dream. Halla, though she did not like to very much, let him have her cloak for one night; she herself slept well enough under his. In the morning he gave her back the dark–blue fold. "Did you get a dream?" she asked. "It smells of you," he said and looked at her deep. But her thoughts were a bear's thoughts. "It is my fur!" she said and took it away from him. After that, as always, morning and evening, they knelt and prayed. Sometimes those in the boat that called themselves Christian knelt and prayed with them. But without Kiot and Roddin it was not the same. And every day they went further north.

There came a time and place when the river boat had discharged and sold all the cargo from the south, Byzantium and beyond, the wine and olives and dried fruit, the woven stuffs, glassware, cups and bowls, and some smaller things of gilt and bronze. They had taken on hides, corn, wool and some goods which had come from far north or east, amber especially. The captain showed them how a piece of amber, rubbed, would catch a fly and in time would eat it up — for see, here was amber with the fleck of a fly deep within it. "It is like God's will," said Tarkan Der, and Halla was not sure what he had in his mind.

But the river boat must turn and go south again, to Olbia, and the things she had loaded would be unloaded and noted by the rats on the quay and then they would be loaded again and go far overseas to Marob and Byzantium. And those who would go further by the east way must either go with a small slow boat on the shallowing river or overland, and they must lose no time, for autumn was coming and the time of snow and the bears' sleep and no travelling. Tarkan Der had still some money left, for the others had left him with almost all they had. It was Greek money, gold, with the little, ugly image of the Purple–born, and they weighed it in careful scales, both sides watching, against weights which they had agreed were just.

So he hired horses and they went the next part of their journey in a caravan, from one stopping place to the next. Tarkan Der talked as well as he could with the other men about weapons, war and hunting, and the customs of the cities and the laws of Holmgard, which were strict and full of justice and a keeping of peace and respect for a bargain made. It would have been easier to talk if Halla had interpreted, but most of the time he did not ask her to, and she rode behind the men and talked to herself or to any other being they might happen to come across. These horses, overworked, hired to one master after another and treated as things, had little to say. But there were cranes and herons circling who had news of a kind, and sometimes beavers, though they were much too busy for light conversation, since logs of wood were their treasure and their plans all to do with the getting of it.

But once she came across a small basilisk dozing in the dry grass and woke it up by gently pulling its tail. It swiveled its eye round at once and gazed at her, but either it was not sufficiently powerful or for some reason Halla was unaffected. It complained of the weather and, when Halla advised it to fly south into the hot sun again, it complained still more that its old stamping grounds were full of men and women who had no respect for basilisks. Even when they migrated into the Egyptian deserts, they had found hermits who exorcised them, most uncomfortably, and made their eyes useless for days. It stretched one of its wings, of such a familiar kind that Halla felt bound to ask it if it had seen any dragons while it was up in the north. "Not so much as a salamander," answered the basilisk sadly, "nothing fiery." However, Halla paid little attention to this, since basilisks are well known to have bad sight for anything but enemies. Yet sometimes she felt she would like some dragon news.

If she dropped behind too much, the men would turn and shout at her. When she told Tarkan Der about the basilisk, he was worried, almost angry with her. It was as though he did not want her to be the kind of woman who talked to basilisks. So after that she sat quiet at the end of the day's march north. Every day brought them a little nearer Holmgard. Every evening they came to a new place, and unsaddled, watered and tethered the horses, made fires, heated water and cooked for themselves. Sometimes there would be some kind of shelter, built for the caravans, and sometimes only an open place.

At night the wild beasts howled and yapped all round them, smelling food, saying: "Dare we? Dare we?" The men took it in turns to guard the camps; once Tarkan Der killed a wolf. But the travellers were yet more afraid of other men. It was against them that they watched, against that the arrows were ready beside bows.

The days grew shorter and the nights colder. They hurried as much as they could, watching the sky. The winds seemed to come from some icy place, cutting on hands and faces, tearing at cloaks. The country was all flat and sometimes they went a difficult way through marshes, strung out singly. But the way was known to the leader of the caravan who had been through the marshes many times. And in the end they came on a river, almost like the river they had left, but flowing north, the same way that they were going. So they said goodbye to their horses and took to a boat again. By the time he had paid for their food on board for the days until they came to Holmgard, Tarkan Der had no money and had sold one of the two gold bosses from his belt.

There had been some rainstorms and the river was swirling down in a brown heavy rush that swept the boat along; the water seemed solider than the planks. The banks were brown too, not high, but yet not so low that they could see the flat beyond them. At night they tied up, for it was dangerous to go on in the dark: but even so it would only be a few days before they were at Holmgard. "What will you do there?" asked Halla.

"I will take service with the Prince of Holmgard," he said, "and there will be a priest there, so we will be married."

"Why shall we be married?" asked Halla, watching the river water looping and spinning on its way north.

"Because it is not right that we should travel together always and not be married," said Tarkan Der.

"Perhaps I will not travel with you always," said Halla.

"We will not always travel. I shall be paid for

my service. We will find a house in Holmgard. A small warm house. I will buy you things for our house as soon as I have money. And things for yourself. You will like to live in a small house with me."

"I do not know at all," whispered Halla, half to him and half to the crooked water. She thought that she could have liked a cave, a cave with a sparkle of treasure deep in its mossy windings. Did he mean he would bring treasure into the house? No, he did not mean that, he was no more a dragon than he was a hero. What was he, then, so close to her, but not herself ? Why was he sure she would like living in a little house? She could have liked a den, safe under rocks and fir branches, the smell of one's den coming richly over the snow and Matulli–bear, her nurse, waiting to lick her to sleep with a hot tickle of tongue. But would a house feel the same? Did All–Father mean her to live in a house? No one can travel light with a house on their back, not even a snail.

Now they were tied up again to the bank, where there was a creek coming down. In the dusk they could see the lights of a few houses at the head of the creek. Someone in the boat said it was a well–doing settlement with a big house and some smaller ones, crops and cattle. They were hospitable folk there, especially Modolf, Otkell's son, who had the big house; his people had come from the north to Holmgard, like many others, and he had settled on the rich land by the river bank, a day's ride from Holmgard. If

this had been day time they would have gone up
to Modolf's hall and asked for milk, and most
likely got meat and bread with it. For this was
the manner of folk they were.

So all in the boat were talking of this and that
and wrapping themselves in cloaks and blankets,
ready for sleep. It was a dark night. And in the
dark night was suddenly screaming like a knife in
the ear. Everyone in the boat woke and listened.
Someone said this must surely be an attack on
the settlement and the pity it was since these
were kindly people and Modolf the best of men,
but it was no use at all to be good unless you
could defend yourself. And now came the red of
fire leaping into the dark sky and a black roof
against it, and the boat's crew thinking it might
be better to cast off and not risk being seen by
the raiders. But Tarkan Der said, "I am going up
to help these folk and perhaps if I do it will stand
in well for me with the Prince of Holmgard. Who
else comes?" So at that a dozen other of the men
said yes, they would come. Halla did not say so,
but she came all the same, following after the
men.

They jumped out into the mud of the creek
as quietly as they could and up the bank, and
ran towards the fire with their swords drawn.
The first man they saw had a reaping hook in
his hand and a bleeding gash all down his face,
and he could hardly stand, but he pointed to
where a man with a great beard and a mail coat
that shone in the flame–light was dragging a
girl along by her wrists, and she was screaming

and her long hair was trailing after her. The girl arched herself forward and bit the man's hand, and as he turned to smash her teeth in Tarkan Der stabbed him in the throat and he fell over in a great mess of blood. Tarkan Der picked up the girl and she was on her knees in front of him, crying bitterly and pointing to the great house. They had tied her father Modolf to his own hall pillar and fired the house round him.

There was fighting for a short time everywhere, but the followers of the bearded man began to break and run, for they could not tell how many were against them. With the tail of her eye Halla saw a Valkyrie plunge out of the night like a shooting star and pick up the bearded one and carry him off on her horse, so she knew he must have been a hero. Then she was standing by Tarkan Der and the men from the boat and the men and women from the settlement and they were all staring at the big house and horribly quiet, and Tarkan Der was holding back the girl who wanted to run in. But it was too late. The flames had taken everywhere and the women of the settlement were beginning to wail, for they had all loved the old man, who had been so just and kindly, and the girl's face was smeared with tears as she tried to tear herself away from the hands that held her.

But Halla was afraid of no flames. Had not the dragons licked her with their forked–flame tongues, dancing in triumph above her through the star–flamed night? Lightly she ran to where the doorbeam had crashed down among lumps of blazing straw, streaming with white–hot flames, wriggling heat of a familiar kind. She jumped it, hearing behind her Tarkan Der yelling her own name desperately. But he would not have understood if there had been time to tell him.

At the far end she saw what she wanted, an old man tied to the pillar of his own high seat, his mouth bleeding where his enemies had struck him, his body huddled forward a little, coughing in the smoke, his mind blurring so that he hardly knew if it was a human who cut the thongs at his back. Halla had been thinking quickly. All very well for herself, but how to get this one out? But as he came into better air he pointed to one corner where the house seemed not to have caught; he leant on her, gasping, as she pulled him over to it. There was a small window, high up. She pushed a table under it and they climbed. But, looking out, there was thatch blazing just where he must fall.

She was not giving up, all the same. She saw two pails of buttermilk standing where they had been left, ran for them and threw them one after another on to the blaze, then in the moment of quieted flame threw down her cloak and pushed the old man through. Then she jumped herself and tugged him clear, pulling the cloak after her. But now there were other hands helping. She saw the girl and Tarkan Der and they were kneeling at her feet and Tarkan Der calling her by the old name, Halla Godsgift. But she began to cry, leaning on his shoulder. Fire–proofed she was, surely, but she had sprained her ankle jumping out of the window and now it had started hurting her.

14

THE STORY

here was no going back to the boat that night. All crowded into an unburnt house: there was bread and meat and milk and honeycombs. Some of the people in the settlement had been killed and wounded, and the raiders had destroyed plenty. But they had been beaten off, the houses would be rebuilt, the cows would calve again. There was enough meal and grain left to see them through winter and the spring sowing. And above all they had back Modolf, the man they loved and honoured, and the girl Alfeida, shaken and still sometimes sobbing, but unhurt. None of the men from the boat had been wounded to speak of, and now the rest of the crew came up. It was decided that they should go on the next day to Holmgard and tell the prince how his laws had been broken and his subjects injured, only a day's ride from the city. There were all too many wandering heroes and raiders, looking for whatever they could lay hands on, younger sons of the great men, with good blood in them,

doubtless, but without patience or honesty, and turning quickly to wickedness and violence if they did not get all they wanted.

Most of the folk in the settlement were signed Christians, and would go to Holmgard at Easter for the three days of sorrow and then gladness. So, when Tarkan Der told them that Halla was a kind of angel who had been sent to him and his friends when they were in trouble, and who could speak all tongues, they believed him. He had to make do at speaking their tongue himself, because Halla had fallen asleep after the women had bandaged her ankle and given her hot milk with some herbs in it. But Modolf and Alfeida and one or two others could speak Greek, and if he and they all spoke slowly they could make do. Everyone was looking at Halla now. While she slept the women combed back her hair, miraculously unsinged, and cut a small secret lock of it here or there to keep for their children's children, who would hear the story told, winter after winter.

But, before he too slept, Tarkan Der thought to himself that now he would surely be able to take honourable service with the Prince of Holmgard. And he thought also that Halla had become different again. How could he have thought of marrying a Godsgift? And yet he had seen her cook and clean; she had washed his shirts for him, after the way of women. She did not do any of these things well, as a girl should who had been brought up in a careful household by a good mother, and he knew all that, and when he was going to marry her he had weighed it and found it did not matter to him at all. What was she then? He knew the smell of her hair and body as well as he knew the smell of his own clothes. He knew the feel of her small shoulders with his arm round them. And yet, yet, he had thought of her in a different way from the way he had been used to think of Sweetfeather, his own. It would have been a different future from the one he had known he would have with Sweetfeather. And both... both were lost. But the future with Halla, had it ever been real? Oh, what was she then, what at all was she, Halla, his travelling friend, his helper, what was she? And he fell on sleep turning this over in his mind and no answer getting.

Halla herself slept on until late the next day, and when she woke her ankle was less swollen. The people in the settlement had begun to get things redded up. Only the smell of burnt wood and thatch hung nastily in the air, clogging the breath. As they pulled out beams which were only half burnt and might serve again for something, or scraped away the hot ashes to see if there was anything left under them, the smoke rose again. Most metal had been spoiled by the heat, would break, but might be taken into Holmgard, melted down again and re–tempered by the smiths there who had great skill. Cattle and horses had their burns dressed as well as men and women. A woman whose labour had come on before time in the middle of the fighting, gave birth safely to a boy. A house of wattles and mud was planned to take the place of the big hall, for this winter at least. Already some of the men had brought back bundles of willows from the river bank. In the evening all gathered again, and work went on at the making of these hurdles by the smoky light of resin torches.

The girl Alfeida had slept too, and now what had happened was beginning to fade into a past nightmare, as the bruises on her scalp and body would fade. All that mattered was the ending of it. She was young. She sat looking at Tarkan Der as he sat cleaning his sword slowly and carefully; she looked at the embroidered pattern of shells on his Marob coat; there was a bit coming loose. Could she ask to mend it, could she take the warm coat off his body and have it in her hands? Halla Godsgift, Halla the angel, she would not want to mend that coat?

Now and then Tarkan Der looked at Alfeida. She was a golden–haired girl and the bruises stood out sharply blue on her white arms and neck; the blood came and went hotly on her cheeks. But the thought of Sweetfeather was on him heavily again. He fell into long, sore silences. It was nothing to him then what he had done at this place.

One of the women was talking to Halla, shyly at first, and then, when she forgot that Halla might be an angel, with all the pleasure that one has at telling old news to a new face. She told her about Alfeida, how she was the old man's only child. Yes, there had been two sons, but one had been killed in a hunting accident and the other had been drowned during the spring floods one year. In spite of the goodness of Modolf, there had been bad luck on the family. It went back far, far, and God in His goodness and wisdom had not seen fit to lift it. The girl Alfeida, too, was a good and kind one, clever at healing, quick at the loom, a lucky hand for butter, a good housewife. It had been most terrible for them all to see her being dragged off by the raiders, they knew for what. Two men had been killed trying to save her. And this one who had rescued her... what kind was he? Where did he come from? What was he thinking to do now? So Halla and the woman spoke away together through the busy, smoky–smelling evening, and it seemed altogether good to Halla if Tarkan Der would want to marry the girl Alfeida instead of herself.

They went the next day to see the laying out of the new house. Alfeida had gone down with the men, was pacing out the walls, marking the corners; she had a straight eye and she knew what was wanted. After a time Tarkan Der had gone down to look and then got interested, and now was helping her. It had taken longer for Modolf to pull himself together, but by the second day he too was rested. He sat down on a hillock, a stick in his hand which he had leant on heavily, coming even this short distance, and a bandage round his wrist where it had been scorched. This strange one, Halla Godsgift, had said she would come out here later, but she too needed to walk with a stick. Was she or was she not a woman? Whose daughter could she be? He watched his own daughter now; she was holding one end of a rope and this man from the south the other; the pegs were hammered in. Then the man looked round, gave the end of the rope to a man from the settlement and walked back to where Halla was making her way over from the hut. He picked her up and carried her up the little hill, the plaits of her unsinged hair falling over his arm. Now she was sitting beside Modolf and Tarkan Der standing by her.

"We had lived in peace for five years," Modolf said. "I thought the arm of the prince was long enough. I thought the luck had turned."

"They were speaking to us, below in the huts, of old ill luck that had been with your folk," said Halla. She too was watching the laying out of the building hurdles, and how the girl Alfeida was showing the men just how things should go.

"It comes from a great way back," said Modolf, and sighed and fretted in the dust with the point of his stick. "In those days my fathers were kings of a kind up north. It is said that there were giants in the world then, giants and dragons."

"But dragons there are, yes, and giants!" said Halla, and she was beginning to feel an odd kind of anxiety, as though this hillock above the river were not a real place at all. She caught Tarkan Der round the ankle and held on to him tight; his hand came down in a friendly and familiar way on to her head.

"In the same way, perhaps, that there are angels and other good spirits, my child," said Modolf, "but as seldom seen. Though now, none of us know what we have seen." He fell silent for a moment, then he went on, "Great wickedness would be done in those days and the white Christ had not come to the north. Men went by ways of old Gods or not of any Gods, but by the violent wills of kings who were their own law. And it is said that a certain king had a wife who died, and he married again. And there was a child of the first wife, a baby girl, and the second wife said that it must be cast out into the forest and die. And so it was done. And my forefathers and I, God help us, through no fault of our own, are children of that king and that wicked queen. But there has been a continuous punishment and the sins of the fathers visited upon the children. Time and again death and destruction have come, lightning has struck, ships have been lost, the enemy has come in the night. First the kingdom was lost, though it was only a little kingdom between mountains and deep woods. And my forefathers came south and east, sometimes setting up a hall and settlement and all going well for a matter of years, sometimes serving as captains to greater kings and princes, such as the Prince of Holmgard, whom my father Otkell served and whom I served as a young man. My father's father was baptised; surely the curse might have lifted then! But always the end was bad and now Alfeida, my daughter, is the last, the very last of the line."

"But the bad luck was lifted from you both," said Halla, "by Tarkan Der — and me." She had begun to breathe again, to know that at least she had not melted away like a reflection from the surface of the water. She must speak, must hear herself speaking. She felt the bones of Tarkan Der's ankle under her hand and her own ankle still aching. Surely they were made of the same flesh and blood!

"If I could believe that was so—" said Modolf slowly.

"I have never known this one to tell lies," said Tarkan Der, looking straight ahead of him and thinking out the words in this speech which was not too easy for him. He added, "And she would know."

"It was a strange thing," Modolf said, "that the curse held for so long, and all for the death of one small child. Worse things have been done than that. Yes, much worse. Yet perhaps the death of the very innocent always carries a curse."

"Perhaps she did not die," said Halla, "perhaps her nurse turned into a bear and carried her away into the forest. Perhaps she was brought up by bears and dragons. Perhaps it was better for her in the end than being a king's child."

"That was never the story," said Modolf.

"Forget the story," said Halla.

Then the girl Alfeida came running up the hill and back to them. "I have told the men to be cutting rushes all tomorrow," she said, "I think there are willows enough. We will have the cows in at the sheltered side — I must get new milk-pails, Father, but there is some ash-wood split — and we shall manage well enough. I think the friends who came to our help should be with us all winter. If they can live in so poor a house, knowing it will be better later—" She dropped her eyes and blushed. Her father repeated it. Yes, surely they must stay.

"I had a thought," said Tarkan Der, "that I would take service with the Prince of Holmgard."

"Take service with me," said Modolf, "and take whatever else you will." And now he was looking straight at his daughter.

"If she says—" said Tarkan Der and leant down towards Halla, knelt beside her, held her a moment close to him, "She is wise."

"I think you must stay here," said Halla.

"And you?"

"I am not sure yet, I am not sure," said Halla with near tears in her voice. "And I do not want to think about it now."

15.

TRAVEL LIGHT

he next day the Prince of Holmgard came riding over, looking very fine indeed in this great quilted coat sewn with scale armour, his sword, ruby–set scabbard, his bearskin and high boots and spiked helmet. Behind came a hundred men of his paid army, whom he used to keep the peace of Holmgard. They were like enough to Varangians. Heroes, no doubt, many of them, thought Halla, regarding them from the hillock where she sat safely alone, while Modolf and Tarkan Der stood by the stirrup of the prince and told him all that had happened.

The prince looked favourably at Tarkan Der, asking him from where he had come, and why, and, after he had heard, the prince invited him to join his paid army. But if he cared to wait here in the settlement until spring, that would be acceptable. "For I am certain you will have the best of hospitality here," the prince said. And then he asked which way the raiders had gone and he spoke to the captain of his hundred bidding him take a half of the men and go hunting the raiders. For the peace of Holmgard must be upheld. If it were not upheld on land, then the next thing might be raiders attacking the trading boats and the caravans, and this must not be, for it was on them and the tolls they paid and the money that was spent by them, that the prosperity of Holmgard rested. And if any prince could not keep the peace, then the people of Holmgard sounded the great bell and called their assembly, did away with such a prince, and put in another instead of him.

So, with this prince's favour on him, all seemed to be well for Tarkan Der and in time he would stop jagging himself on the memory of Sweetfeather and Marob. In time he would forgive his enemies and would forgive Byzantium for not being what he thought it would be. He would think happily of his young brother Yillit taking his place in Marob and never go back and find out what had really happened. The two rivers were between him and the past. Alfeida would be between him and the past. He had been a traveller, but now he was coming to a stop. And it will be a happy place for him, thought Halla, but I — I have not come to a place where my travelling should stop. There is no reason here that I can find to keep me. And I am still myself, and what tricks at all did All–Father play on me?

So there she sat for a while and below the hillock to one side was the square of the new house laid out in hurdles, but she turned her back on it. On the other side of the hillock there

were alders and marsh between her and a bend
of the river, and clumps of high rushes and old
broken willows that were no use for wattles
or any other thing. But there was something
moving down there among them. Watching, she
hunched her cloak round her, for she was a
little cold. Then slowly she got to her feet and
walked down that way, limping still, but not
too much. It was certainly not the cattle of the
settlement down there. Was it wild beasts? She
went cautiously. And then she saw a great wing
suddenly stretching from behind a tree. It must
be a Valkyrie, perhaps several of them, Steinvor
and the girls. She put a finger in her cheek and
whistled. At once there was quiet, in an instant
the wing had furled itself out of sight as though
it had never been. But a minute afterwards
Steinvor ducked under a low alder bough and
came up to where Halla stood. "So it's you, dear.
I might have guessed."

"Yes," said Halla, "it's me. At least I suppose
it's me. But they told me something — Steinvor,
are there any giants about now?"

"Well," said Steinvor, "now that I come to think
of it, I haven't seen any giants lately. But they
must be somewhere. After all, Halla, they're to
be our enemies in the Last Battle. It wouldn't do
at all if the battle was to start and there were no
enemies."

"If you ask me," said Halla, "I'd say it would be
just like one of All–Father's little jokes. And what
about dragons?"

"Oh, I suppose there are dragons about still.

152

Not as many as there used to be, certainly. Not here. I expect you'd find plenty in China. Or Arabia. Only not just round the corner, the way there were once."

"What happened to all their treasures?"

"I think men have begun to behave dragonishly about treasure," said Steinvor, frowning and fidgeting with her belt buckle. "You know, even the heroes don't seem to give it away in the openhanded way they used to. Perhaps they and the dragons have got to understanding one another so well that there are no quarrels between them now."

"Yes," said Halla, "yes. It is difficult to keep one's enemies. That must make it awkward for the Gods and the giants. Perhaps they came to understand one another too. If they did there'll be no Last Battle, and what will you do with all those heroes?" Steinvor shook her head: that was too much! Halla went on, "How long ago was it, Steinvor, that you came to Dragon Mountain and talked to me?"

"Well, I've been so busy, what with one thing and another," said Steinvor, and began re–plaiting her hair, which was as red as ever. "Time slips by, you'd not know yourself! A few years back, wasn't it?"

"How many years? Five years? Five hundred years? Steinvor, you know what I mean. What kind of game has All–Father been having with me?"

"What did he say to you, Halla?"

"He said, Travel Light."

"If you did that, if you travelled light, you might travel through the years and travel faster than some. Would you have it otherwise, Halla?"

"I think he might have told me."

"He never tells us, Halla. We have to find out. Why not come with us for a bit?"

"I told you before, Steinvor, I don't like heroes."

"They're getting very rare. In fact, we're all here because there's going to be a bit of luck for us. A fight between the prince's army and those raiders. Almost sure to be several heroes. But, believe it or not, sometimes we'll be cruising for months and never get a chance. All over the place, too. Mountains, you've no idea!"

"I haven't seen a mountain since… since… It's all flat between here and Micklegard. Marshes. And these rivers without any rocks in them."

"One evening we were all taking off from a crag in the Caucasus. And the sun setting away below. Of course, that's the kind of thing these horses enjoy."

"I like horses," said Halla softly and took a short step forward.

"Ours have much more conversation than most horses," said Steinvor, "more point of view, you know. In fact, they argue sometimes."

"Would there be a horse for me?" Halla asked.

"All–Father wished them for us. If he wished one for you — yes, look, that lovely grey with the black points, he's new!"

"All–Father might have told me," said Halla, hesitating still. But it was a beautiful horse, so beautiful, something like a unicorn but more intelligent looking, its great wings arching and quivering, better than a real horse, better than a ship. Riding on that horse you would need nothing, no cloak even. She dropped it on the edge of the marshland. Nothing. You could travel light.

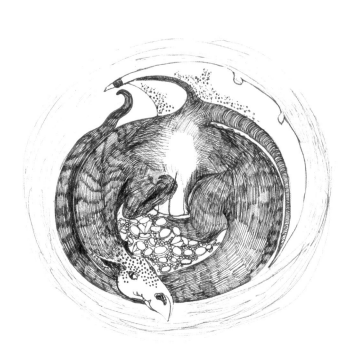

GLOSSARY

All–Father
A supreme god in Norse mythology also known as Odin. He is associated with wisdom, magic and prophecy.

Andromeda
In Greek mythology, Andromeda was a princess that was chained to a rock as a sacrifice to the sea monster/dragon Cetus.

Basilisk
Legendary king of snakes, the basilisk is said to be incredibly venomous, and has the power to freeze its enemies in place with a single glance.

Bower
A woman's bedroom or chambers in a medieval castle (derived from the French word *boudoir*).

Byzantium
A city in Ancient Greece, later called Constantinople, today known as Istanbul (in Turkey). Also referred to in the text as Mickelgard.

Corn King
A mythical character appointed king for a year before being sacrificed to help the crops.

Crowberry
A small evergreen shrub, found on moorlands and in spruce forests. It bears a fruit similar to a blueberry.

Crupper
A leather strap that is looped under a horse's tail to prevent the saddle sliding forward.

Dragon Ships
Viking ships that were decorated with a dragon's head.

Fenris Wolf
Based on Fenrisulfr from Norse mythology. It was prophesised that the wolf would devour Odin (the All–Father) in the Last Battle.

Fjords
A long, narrow inlet with steep sides, created by glaciers.

George and the Dragon
Legend tells of how St. George slayed a plague–bearing dragon in Libya to rescue the king's daughter and to convert the natives to Christianity.

Goddess Demeter
The Greek Goddess of the Bountiful Harvest.
Renowned for her generosity and thought to be
responsible for plentiful crops.

Hippodrome
A type of stadium used by the Greeks for
chariot and horse racing.

Holmgard
Varangian name for the city of Novgorod (in
Russia). Varangians were Vikings who lived in
the 9th and 10th centuries.

Igneous
The oldest type of all rocks, the term "igneous"
comes from a Latin word meaning fire.

Kiev
The capital city of Ukraine.

Lapis
A bright blue semi–precious stone found in
places such as Afghanistan and Siberia.

Last Battle
Also known as Ragnarök (the final destiny
of the gods). When all the major gods, such
as Odin, will perish and the world will be
submerged under water.

Malachite
A green mineral found in many places, including Russia, Zambia, Mexico, Australia and France.

Martyr
Someone who dies for a cause or for his/her beliefs.

Middle Sea
Mediterranean Sea, also called the Great Sea.

Midgard Serpent
Also known as Jormungand. The All–Father threw the serpent into the ocean that encircles Midgard (one of the Nine Worlds that contains humans). The serpent was said to grow so large it was able to surround the Earth and grasp its own tail — when it lets go the world will end.

Norns
Female beings in Norse mythology that control destiny.

Northern Lights
Also known as the aurora borealis, these are bright lights in the sky which can be seen in far–north places such as the North Pole.

Olbia
A town in Sardinia, an island off the west coast of Italy.

Perseus
Hero in Greek mythology who killed monsters
including Medusa, and rescued Andromeda.

Pharisees
A party of Jews who around 140–37 BC formed
in opposition to a group called the Sadducees.

Phoenix
A mythical bird that is said to burst into flames
at the end of its life; from the ashes a new
phoenix rises.

Pigsticking
Another name for boar hunting, using a
specialised boar spear.

Pole Star
Also known as the North Star, usually the
brightest star in the sky.

Porphyry
A purple–red coloured rock made up of
crystals.

Pyre
A structure made of wood used for cremation
during funerals.

River Dnieper
Ukraine's largest river, it flows from Russia to
the Black Sea.

Scythians
An ancient race of Iranian people.

Sea Serpent
A type of mythical sea monster, also called a sea dragon.

Valhalla
The Viking heaven for those who have died in battle.

Valkyrie
Valkyries decide who dies in battle and take those Vikings to Valhalla.

Wanderer
A warrior who has lost his fellow fighters, his lord and his home. He walks by himself and is often used by Odin as a disguise.

Yggdrasil
A huge tree in Norse mythology which is very important to the gods. There are nine worlds surrounding Yggdrasil.

LAST WORD

We hope that you have enjoyed reading this book and that Halla, the dragons and the landscapes live on in your imagination.

You may have wondered who created this edition of *Travel Light*. The answer is simple — it is the product of a team of postgraduate students who wanted to bring an undiscovered classic back to life. The project was carried out by the staff and students of MSc Publishing at Edinburgh Napier University within the Scottish Centre for the Book (SCOB).

Over the course of the year–long Masters programme the students learned all about the publishing industry, and even had a taste of what it is like to work in this creative and exciting environment. They developed design skills and examined individual companies and their operations to give them a better understanding of the marketplace. One project on which the students worked was *Buzz* magazine, with their learning expanding from theory to practice. For their other live project, the students were given the challenge of re–launching an existing title. The book you now hold in your hand is the end product of that journey.

Travel Light is a wonderful, exciting book. The students hope that you will read and re–read it, passing it on to friends with the same sense of excitement. It was unanimously chosen from a shortlist of books. Everyone felt that this book could be as popular as titles such as *The Lord of the Rings* and *Harry Potter*. The students also wanted to bring a talented Scottish author to the attention of new generations of Scottish readers.

Naomi Mitchison was born in Edinburgh in 1897. She wrote over 90 works, more than 70 of which were novels, their genres ranging from history to science fiction. She was an avid traveller and was influenced by other cultures in her writings. She even became a tribal mother to the people of Bakgatla (a tribe in Botswana). Since her death in 1999 (at the age of 101) she has remained in print but her reputation has begun to fade. It was one of the students' aims to ensure that her work continued to be read by new readers.

Once the book had been decided upon, the students conducted market research. The results showed that *Travel Light* should be targeted at P6 and P7 pupils. The students then sent sample pages to primary schools, asking for feedback from both teachers and pupils, in order to determine the most suitable format and design for this age group.

The text of *Travel Light* has been edited to ensure that it is as accurate as possible and any obscure words, including those relating to

Norse mythology, are defined in a glossary. The striking illustrations on the cover of the book and its inner pages were contributed by William B. Hill, an up–and–coming young Scottish illustrator. We think his beautiful cover image really conveys the nature of the novel and will appeal to a young readership.

Travel Light is one of the first children's titles to be produced by Merchiston Publishing. The students decided that it needed a different look from that of its predecessors in order to appeal to a new market. So they altered its size and format.

As the production process developed, the students requested quotations from a number of printers and chose one on the basis of value for money and quality. Finally, they had to present the new *Travel Light* to their lecturers and industry professionals as part of their assessment. The readers, however, are the real judges of any book and we hope this one receives your positive approval.

This project has been supported by the Edward Clark Bequest, which has its origins in the will of Edward Clark. He was the Chairman and Managing Director of R. & R. Clark Ltd of Edinburgh — an important printer in its day serving all the major publishers and authors of the late nineteenth and early twentieth centuries. Edward Clark wished his legacy to be used specifically for the benefit of students involved in printing and publishing. We are grateful to the Trustees for honouring his wishes and offering financial support for the production of *Travel Light*.

The publishing courses at Edinburgh Napier University began over 40 years ago, and our graduates now hold key positions in the publishing industry worldwide. There is a strong sense of tradition here at Napier but we also pride ourselves on our innovation and creativity. If you wish to learn more about what we have to offer or about the production of *Travel Light*, please have a look at our website www.merchistonpublishing.com or contact us by e–mail at scob@napier.ac.uk.

Professor Alistair McCleery

Edinburgh Napier University
MSc Publishing students

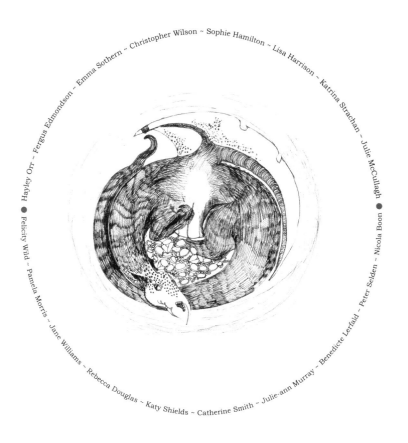

Christopher Wilson ~ Sophie Hamilton ~ Lisa Harrison ~ Katrina Strachan ~ Julie McCullagh ~ Nicola Boon ~ Peter Selden ~ Benedicte Lerfald ~ Julie-ann Murray ~ Catherine Smith ~ Katy Shields ~ Rebecca Douglas ~ Jane Williams ~ Pamela Morris ~ Felicity Wild ~ Hayley Orr ~ Fergus Edmondson ~ Emma Sothern ~